"You're the disguise master. Any suggestions?"

"You've never wanted to take the suggestions I made a few weeks ago, Samantha. Why ask me now?" Daniel's eyes bored into her, demanded answers she didn't want to face.

"I only–"

"Only what? You told me you could manage anything Finders, Inc. handed you. You accused me of misjudging you, of refusing to acknowledge your abilities. And a whole lot of other things." His amber eyes glittered hard, cold. "I'm only here because you said you needed help."

Meaning she'd proven she wasn't able to handle this case on her own. If only she'd never said it, never uttered those horrible words. Sam had only counted on hurting him as he'd hurt her. What she hadn't considered was that Daniel wouldn't forgive her.

"You're in charge here, Sam. What do you want to do?"

"I don't know yet. But I'll figure it out...."

Books by Lois Richer

Love Inspired Suspense

A Time To Protect #13
††*Secrets of the Rose* #27
††*Silent Enemy* #29

Love Inspired

A Will and a Wedding #8
†*Faithfully Yours* #15
†*A Hopeful Heart* #23
†*Sweet Charity* #32
A Home, a Heart,
a Husband #50
This Child of Mine #59
**Baby on the Way* #73
**Daddy on the Way* #79
**Wedding on the Way* #85
‡*Mother's Day Miracle* #101
‡*His Answered Prayer* #115
‡*Blessed Baby* #152
Tucker's Bride #182
Inner Harbor #207
***Blessings* #226
***A Time To Remember* #256
Past Secrets, Present Love #328

†Faith, Hope & Charity
*Brides of the Seasons
‡If Wishes Were Weddings
**Blessings in Disguise
††Finders Inc.

LOIS RICHER

Sneaking a flashlight under the blankets, hiding in a thicket of Caragana bushes where no one could see, pushing books into socks to take to camp—those are just some of the things Lois Richer freely admits to in her pursuit of the written word. "I'm a book-a-holic. I can't do without stories," she confesses. "It's always been that way."

Her love of language evolved into writing her own stories. Today her passion is to create tales of personal struggle that lead to triumph over life's rocky road. For Lois, a happy ending is essential.

LOIS RICHER

SILENT ENEMY

Published by Steeple Hill Books™

STEEPLE HILL BOOKS

ISBN-13: 978-0-373-87389-0
ISBN-10: 0-373-87389-1

SILENT ENEMY

This edition published by arrangement with Steeple Hill Books.

www.SteepleHill.com

Printed in U.S.A.

We are pressed on every side by troubles,
but not crushed and broken. We are perplexed
because we don't know why things happen as they
do, but we don't give up. We are hunted down,
but God never abandons us. We get knocked down,
but we get up again and keep going.

—*II Corinthians* 4:8–9

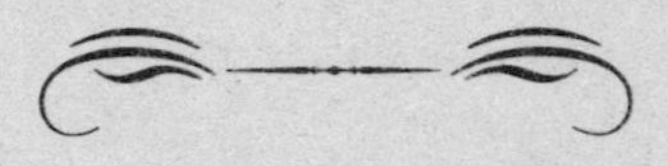

This book is lovingly dedicated
to the men and women around the globe who
sacrifice so much to bring the good news to all
people. Thank you is not enough.

PROLOGUE

"What lies behind us and what lies before us are tiny matters compared to what lies within us."

—Ralph Waldo Emerson

"The shipments came in short last time."

"What would I know about that? I just deliver the merchandise."

"El Señor does not like shortages."

"Then he should talk to his supplier. I'm just the delivery man." He tucked the cello-wrapped packets in under the boxes of supplies, adjusted the load so the tarp covered everything. When all was secure, he went to the office, used the pay phone.

"A small brown box will be waiting for you at the Grand Hotel Bolivia. You know what to do. Fail and you will pay dearly."

"The money?"

"There are a list of stops. You will be paid at each. Don't mess up."

He hung up the phone, poured himself a cup of coffee and spent some time perusing a newspaper. When he saw the tired old car coming, he went back to the plane and adjusted his cargo one more time. Nothing was out of place.

"You have loaded it all?"

"Absolutely everything." He helped the older man into his seat, then slammed the door shut. After radioing the tower, they taxied onto the runway. Soon the tiny plane crested over the rain forest.

"Why don't you continue with your story, Padre?"

By the time he reached the airstrip bordering the compound, he had all the information he needed.

ONE

"*The most effective disguise isn't.*"

Samantha Henderson drew the tattered edges of Bertha-the-street-lady's shawl around her and wondered if her boss had ever been reduced to this.

Not likely.

The slap of footsteps paused, stopped just behind her. She made sure the brim of Bertha's straw hat hid her face.

"Look around. She's got to be here."

Varga!

Sam hunched over, hacked out a loud, chesty cough and turned it into a long-winded rumble that suggested an unhealthy lung condition. After a loud expletive, the feet moved a safer distance away.

"What do I do now? He'll kill me if he finds out I lost her."

"Check the market. If I find her, I'll hang on to her. We've got to be there at four. Now go. El Zopilote doesn't like complications."

Four? Sam checked her watch. She had to be ready to move, and that meant getting rid of this disguise. If that statue was going anywhere, she had to know. That's why she was there.

El Zopilote—The Vulture. Was he the buyer? She'd assumed Varga was a small-time thief, the other guy a pal he'd paid to help. But if they both worked for this el Zopilote…

The wind played with her hat, tugged it against its thin strings. She reached to grab it, noticed Bertha's nod. Time to go.

While Varga had his back turned, Samantha limped over to the black wrought-iron fence that led to a courtyard, one of many in Lima. This one had a bougainvillea tree in full flower—good cover. From here she could look out onto the square. Varga and friend loped across the busy street.

She tossed her hat onto the ground, peeled off her ratty shawl, voluminous skirt and peasant blouse until all she wore were her jeans and T-shirt. Relief from the heat of two layers of clothing swept across her darkened skin. Repeatedly applying the self-tanner had ensured she was as dark as any native Peruvian, but now she needed a new look. She undid her braids, finger-combed her hair loose so that it shielded her face. Now she looked like a tourist.

While unearthing her backpack from the brambles of the tree, Sam peeked through the branches. On the corner across the street, Varga stood speaking to his friend. He had a package tucked under one arm.

So he still had the statue. Sam pulled on her sunglasses, ducked out of her hiding place and ambled down the street to a bench half a block down. She sat, picked up the newspaper and pretended to read. Following Juan Varga wasn't the problem. Figuring out why he did the things he did was. He should have handed the statue over long ago instead of traipsing across South

America. If el Zopilote had something to do with his actions, maybe this four o'clock meeting would give her an opportunity to find out why.

Making informed decisions about her next move was impossible. All she could do was follow Varga and wait for answers. In the meantime, she'd check in. She dialed Finders, Inc. and waited. For the third time in three days she couldn't get through. After several attempts she tried a different number. The phone rang endlessly.

A two-hour time difference between here and the offices in Victoria meant that a certain someone who kept erratic hours should be in to take her call on his private line. Except that Daniel McCullough did not pick up. Either the phone system wasn't working properly or her cell phone was faulty. Both major mistakes for an agent of her experience.

Samantha wasn't where she was supposed to be. In fact she hadn't made contact with another agent since yesterday and that hadn't been through Finders' regular channels. Nothing about this recovery was going according to plan. In desperation, she called a local number she'd been given for emergencies. A nonhuman voice asked her to leave a message.

"This is Samantha Henderson. I'm in Lima, still with Varga, who is smuggling the statue from location to location. No idea why. I tried the office, couldn't get through. Sorry."

Her target was on the move again.

Sam shoved her phone in her pocket, hitched her pack over her shoulder and followed, using the flush of tourists as cover. When he rented a car, she did the same. When Varga climbed on a northbound train, Sam followed, near enough to keep an eye on him, far enough away that most people would think she was part of a tourist group snapping pictures.

Four o'clock came and went as the train chugged in and out of villages, carrying them toward the Andes. When Varga bedded down in his sleeper, Sam kept watch, but her suspicions worked overtime. The man was too casual, as if something had changed, and yet he talked to no one, received no phone calls. He simply rode the train. Three days later she was dirty, tired and fed up when he finally disembarked in Iquitos, doorway to the Amazon.

Varga checked into a hotel long enough to eat, shower and change. Sam bought a new shirt, scrubbed up in the hotel washroom, then waited outside the restaurant until he took off again, across the city this time. When he finally arrived at a small wharf, she tried her phone again, hoping for advice.

"Daniel?"

"Sam? I can hardly hear you."

The line went dead. She hovered near the pay phones, but had barely finished dialing when Varga and two men who'd obviously been waiting for him climbed aboard a vessel and prepared to take off.

Sam edged closer, pretended to negotiate with a fish seller. Varga and company were boisterous, almost jubilant as they prepared to cast off. She couldn't hear everything, but the words el Padre Dulce were repeated several times. It sounded like they were traveling upriver to meet this person. Sam had to follow. The question was how.

As Varga's boat pulled out of the harbor, she made up her mind and approached an older man who was loading boxes onto his flat boat.

"Hola, señor!" In rapid Spanish she asked the man

about el Padre Dulce. He nodded and began gesticulating, explaining that he was taking these gifts from an unknown beneficiary to the padre. Was she, too, traveling to see him?

"*Sí,*" she agreed, smiling widely. The man, Ramon, offered to take her with him. The padre apparently loved visitors. Once the cargo was safely stowed, they were soon chugging down the river.

Ramon had a pair of binoculars that Sam borrowed. Several times she spotted Varga ahead of them. The other boat's erratic speed puzzled her—sometimes they revved far ahead, sometimes they barely moved—until she saw a bottle go flying overboard and realized the men were drinking. Ramon kept his speed steady, pointed out a toucan that stretched overhead. To relax she concentrated on finding species of birds she already knew: capped heron and three species of kingfishers. But her nerves remained tightly strung.

If only she could figure out why Varga was taking this trip.

The humidity added to her growing misgivings as the river drew them along its coiling, rasping course. The jungle, lush and teeming with life, hung on either side—beautiful, lowering, and filled with foreboding shadows. Every so often a waterfall cascaded down a smooth rock face in staircases carved by time.

The waning afternoon light moved in cubes as the forest grew thicker, bushy, dense and even more humid. Still the boats chugged along. With nothing else to do, Sam harked back to that conversation in Daniel's office.

You can't be a loner. You have to follow the rules, Samantha. Just like everyone else. And that includes reporting in, no matter where you are.

She grimaced, pulled out her phone and dialed Finders, Inc. again. "It's me. I've left Lima and am—hello?" They'd been cut off. "So much for your rules, Daniel."

She slid the phone closed, but a moment later reopened it and dialed again, this time to the routing service Finders had set up to pass on messages from their agents in the field.

"I'm following the statue, as ordered," she said, after identifying herself. "Varga has been joined by two men. I think they work for el Zopilote, whoever that is. Please investigate that name, see if you can find some background. I believe he's the one who's giving the orders, or perhaps buying the statue from Varga."

Daniel would be surprised she was adhering to his rules so closely, but she wanted that promotion. She tucked the phone back into the pocket of her jeans, leaned against some boxes, constantly scanning the area. Every pore of her body sensed a threat—silent for now, but present nonetheless.

Ramon shared his bread and cheese with her, assured her they were on the right path to this el Padre's place. Five hours later they finished the last of his sodas. What seemed like aeons after that the motor began to sputter. Sam's misgivings escalated when her phone showed no signal. She had no means of telling anyone exactly where she was.

When the sputtering grew worse, Ramon steered toward shore and shut the motor off. She could hear the steady put-putting of the other boat not far ahead. At least she hadn't lost them. Yet.

"What's wrong?"

Ramon poked and probed the motor. "*El carburador.*" Carburetor. He grinned when the engine coughed to life.

Given the amount of black smoke they were spewing,

Sam worried the other boat would come back to investigate, but as their boat limped along, hugging the shoreline, she caught glimpses of the other craft. Forest-green turned to gray, then brown, then purple as the sunlight faded.

"Can't you do something?" she begged, peering through the binoculars. She couldn't see or hear Varga's boat.

"I'm sorry, *señorita.* It is an old boat and we must go slowly. Perhaps when we get to el Padre's camp, he will help us."

El Padre Dulce. That name again. *Sweet Father*—an odd title certainly. But Sam wasn't looking to find a priest. She wanted to know why Varga had come here with the statue.

"El Padre Dulce is a good man. All the people here love him very much." Ramon patted the engine with pride. "He helped me buy this boat. He helps many people. Today I am bringing him gifts."

"I'm sure he's wonderful," she agreed. "But I was hoping we would catch up with the other boat."

"All will be well, *señorita.* God cares for his children. Do not worry."

How did you argue with that? As the muddy water slid past, Samantha gave up pretending she was in control. Here on the river she was exposed, vulnerable. Using her GPS, she quickly sent the coordinates to Finders' satellite—just in case. Maybe it was those fingers of dusk creeping down the banks like a stalker, or maybe it was the cackling sound emanating from the forest that freaked her, but her internal radar now switched to high.

The motor coughed, wheezed and then stopped again. Ramon paddled toward the bank.

"*Señorita,* I must work on this motor. It is not much

farther. Perhaps you wish to walk on shore while I work?" Clearly he didn't want her bugging him while he fiddled with the motor.

Since Sam desperately needed some privacy and a bush, she left her backpack on the bench of the boat, climbed over the hull and jumped onto the beach. Ramon watched her for a moment, and then began to quietly hum as he unveiled the inner workings of his machine. Sam chose a secluded area. Five minutes later she emerged from the grove of trees and froze.

The boat was gone. Poor Ramon floated facedown in the water, a knife sticking out of his back.

Sam swallowed her cry, aware that the killer could be very close, waiting for her. Where was Ramon's God now? She'd never believed all that stuff about God loving everyone anyway. She didn't need Him now, either. She'd manage on her own. She was used to that.

Varga, or one of his cohorts must have done this. Ramon had told her the jungle natives of this area were friendly, especially to el Padre Dulce's friends. Ramon had even waved to a tribal group who stood solemnly on shore, watching as they moved past.

Sam listened for several moments. No motor sounds, no laughing voices, nothing but the soft lap of water against the shore. She inventoried her surroundings and made a decision. Without a boat, climbing uphill was the only way to scout out the land. Trampling through the thick ferny undergrowth proved how quickly the light was fading. She reached the uppermost ridge and looked around. Varga's boat lay in a little cove several hundred yards downstream. Ramon's boat was there, too, but the crates and boxes he'd so carefully loaded were missing. She turned around.

A flash of light flickered through the trees. Perhaps the padre's camp was nearer than she thought. Perhaps Varga was already there, exchanging the statue.

Going forward could be dangerous, but going back was impossible. She walked toward the light. Progress through the damp, slippery forest was difficult in loose sandals, but her sneakers were in her backpack, on the boat. She moved carefully, deliberately choosing each step. Five hundred feet along the ridge Samantha suddenly lost her footing and tumbled down the embankment. The world spun round like a crazy kaleidoscope, punctuated by stabs of bright light and darkness. Her head smacked against a rock at the same time that her ribs met resistance against the forest's bulging roots.

Samantha fought to stop herself, but the vines were too slippery. She tumbled farther into the impenetrable darkness until at last she came to rest against something big and hard and damp. Pain rolled in waves over her body. She opened her mouth to cry out, then shut it, remembering Ramon's spread-eagled body floating facedown. A black cloud hovered just above her. She tried to remain awake but her brain wouldn't obey.

With a little sigh, Sam closed her eyes as the truth hit. Daniel was right. She wasn't ready for promotion.

Something was wrong.

Daniel McCullough had built his career around his intuition, had escaped death more than once because he followed his instinct. At the moment it was screaming a warning, but this warning had nothing to do with him.

Samantha.

He jumped as the phone squawked its summons, told himself to get a grip. "Yes?"

"It's Miss Henderson, Daniel. They've tracked her cell. She's called us a number of times. Communications has found messages and some GPS coordinates."

"Let me hear the messages, Evelyn."

"Yes, sir."

A moment later Sam's voice filled the room, quiet, steady, determined. If he closed his eyes, Daniel could see her standing there, her shawl of raven black hair cascading down to her waist, emerald eyes bright, focused and unafraid.

"Sir?"

Daniel blinked, realized his assistant had been waiting for several minutes. "Tape it and bring me a copy. I want someone in communications working on her reports full-time. Investigations should check out this el Zopilote. I want to know who he is, what his interest in the statue is. Make a copy of the tape for them. Ask the lab to distinguish some of the background sounds. And have her GPS signal mapped, will you? If anyone hears anything from Samantha Henderson they are to report immediately to me."

"Yes, sir." Not long after that his assistant returned, placed the tape on his desk, then left.

Daniel picked up the tape, the same old nerve rat-tatting its warning. Over and over he listened to her voice, each time telling himself he was a fool to have let her go, each time wondering if he'd ever get a chance to apologize. He waited impatiently for the first report to arrive and then pored over the map. "You're sure this is right?"

"As far as we can tell she was in the Andes, traveling down the Amazon when she sent it. The signal was weak, but identifiable."

The lab verified that the background sounds were

consistent with canopy birds in the Amazon. But still no one was able to reach Sam on her cell phone. Daniel offered himself the comforts he usually dispensed to others in situations like this. She was fine. She'd call in shortly. It was just a communications glitch. He didn't believe himself.

Investigations were the last to report in. "I'm sorry, sir. We have no one who fits the name el Zopilote. There's nothing in our intelligence files to lead us in any particular direction."

"Keep looking." Daniel chewed his bottom lip while suspicions kept nagging at him—that Samantha Henderson had stepped into a school of piranha.

As CEO of Finders, Inc., Daniel was used to sending agents all over the world to track lost or missing items for its clients. Just because he'd ordered Samantha Henderson to Brazil to recover a statue did not mean she wasn't going to experience problems. In their line of work nothing was ever a sure thing, but that held especially true in Samantha's cases. Wait a minute—he'd sent her to *Brazil,* not Peru.

"You remind me of Grant, all hunched over in your chair, glaring at the desk." Shelby Kincaid-Austen stood in the doorway, watching him.

"Hey, Shel. C'mon in."

Grant Kincaid had been Daniel's commanding officer in Special Ops training. The two had become fast friends when both were assigned to covert work in Malaysia. It was Grant who'd appreciated Daniel's ability at disguise—an ability Daniel had gained from years of practice avoiding news hounds whose stories unfailingly painted Daniel as the heir apparent to McCullough International. Thanks to Grant, Daniel had completed many successful missions pretending to be someone else, someone without a past.

"You're wishing he was here, aren't you?" Shelby asked.

He nodded. Special Ops was ugly, a place Grant had grown tired of after he met Shelby. By then Daniel also wanted a more stable lifestyle, so the three had decided to form their own recovery agency. Finders, Inc. was born. That choice had freed Daniel from the expectations his father's empire had always engendered and allowed him to do his job disguised as anyone he wanted to be.

"Do you wish you could walk away from here, Daniel?" Shelby touched his shoulder. "I'm very grateful you've been running the business since Grant's death, but you don't have to stay at Finders, Inc. You don't owe me or the company a thing. You loved field-work. Would you prefer to go back to it?"

"Not at the moment. Staying in one place for more than a day has benefits." He winked. "The vicarious thrills are easier on this old body than firsthand contact. Don't worry. My life is okay even if it isn't chock-full of a daughter and a new husband," he teased.

"Your life could be very full, Daniel."

She didn't say it but he knew she saw past his facade. Shelby was probably the only person in the whole building who could have guessed he was worried about Sam.

"I'm fine, Shel."

"No, you're not. You coop yourself up in here for eighteen hours a day, worrying about things you can't change. You need to get out once in a while. With someone." Her scolding mother-hen glare challenged him to deny it.

"Maybe." *Been there, done that. Didn't work.* He

changed topics. "I was thinking about Finders' rules. We've only ever had three. Maybe it's time we looked at them again."

"Three are all we need. Complete anonymity for the client. Nothing illegal and every job completed. Why change what works?"

"Maybe they need updating." Maybe someone should be grading him on his ability to judge character, he felt like saying. "After all, we're changing. Tim's on board now. Maybe we need to rethink things."

Daniel stayed at Finders because Shelby had asked him to. He never wanted her to know that sometimes, when everyone went home to their families, he sat in the dark, waiting for news of another success, feeling trapped by the office and its never-ending demands.

He could never tell her he yearned to don one of his disguises and take off, because he knew the temptation to get back to working in the field hid a deeper longing, one that had a lot to do with a certain frustrating brunette who had cast him as the bad guy in her world.

"Don't second-guess yourself, Daniel. You sent Sam because she knows what she's doing."

"I hope so. We've lost communication with her."

"She'll call back." She headed for the door. "It's just a statue, Daniel."

"That was supposed to stay in Brazil," he reminded, but Shelby had already left. Ignoring the sheaves of files loading down his desk, Daniel moved to the glass wall of his office and looked down onto the semicircular floors stacked below, each one housing an integral part of the finely tuned mechanism called Finders, Inc. All this technology and yet…

Sam was fine. Maybe she had needed to go undercover or had a change in plans. Sam knew her job. She was one of the best recovery specialists Finders had ever employed. It was the job she'd applied for that Daniel had been worried about. He'd turned down her request for promotion the same day the Brazil job came up. Samantha's departure from his office had been abrupt, bitter. Daniel regretted what he'd said, but there was no way now to take it back.

"Can I bother you again?"

Daniel blinked at the blurry figure in the doorway, fumbled for his glasses. Shelby. "You're still here?" He squinted at his watch. "Shouldn't you be home with Aimee? Tim checked out a while ago." He glanced at the security monitor on his desk, registered the notation.

"As soon as he comes back, home is where I'm headed. In the meantime, Aimee sent you a gift. I forgot to give it to you this morning." Shelby dropped a picture drawn by her young daughter onto the desk. "She said you'd know what it is."

He moved back to the desk, sat down behind it and picked up the colorful piece of paper. He wanted to groan. Two figures with black capes stood opposite each other holding what Daniel guessed were swords.

"Do you know what it means?"

"Enemies," he explained sheepishly. "When she stopped by last week, Aimee overheard me arguing with someone. That engendered a long discussion about enemies. I guess she's reminding me to forgive and forget."

As if Daniel could ever forget Samantha's words.

You cheated me, Daniel. I can do that job with my hands tied and you know it. He could still see the hurt at the back of her eyes. *Hurting people—you, your father. Is that a McCullough trait?*

"Daniel?"

He blinked, saw Shelby's frown.

"Sorry. Daydreaming." He hid his embarrassment by grabbing Aimee's picture and fixing it to his filing cabinet with a magnet.

"Samantha told me you turned down her application to supervise."

He glanced sideways at her, wondering if he should have run that one past her, but Shelby anticipated his thoughts and shook her head.

"I'm not second-guessing you, Daniel."

"Thanks."

"I know you have to make tough decisions for Finders, but I also know that you're fair. If you think Sam isn't ready for additional responsibility, then I agree."

He should have been relieved by her confidence—instead he wondered if she was mistaken to put so much trust in him.

Shelby's beeper paged. "That's Tim. He's waiting for me. I'd better go." She stepped around the desk, leaned over and hugged him, the touch of her lips brief against his cheek. "Maybe I forget to tell you sometimes but you're doing a great job here, Daniel. Know that Tim and I both appreciate all you've sacrificed to give us the time and space we need in this new marriage."

"I only want to see you happy, Shel. Tim makes you happy. Aimee, too. I'm glad."

"Me, too." She didn't need to say more. Her face glowed. "Good night."

"'Night, Shel." A flicker of envy went through him. His whole life he'd wanted to know how that kind of love felt. It had never happened. Probably never would now. Daniel pushed away the longing, turned back to the computer. He pulled up a map of Brazil, traced Sam's progress from the moment she'd landed in Rio, traveled to Horizonte, then São Paulo. It made no sense to go to Peru. He'd seen no Intel that connected the statue to anyone there.

You don't trust me, Daniel. You never have. Is that because you don't trust yourself?

It wasn't trust that tortured him—it was guilt. His choices had wreaked havoc on his world ever since a day long ago when he'd still been a boy.

Peru. In his mind he heard the thunder of breakers in the surf, smelled the briny salt water, saw pristine white sails unfurl in a freshening wind. His skin grew warm from the tropical sun and he longed to cool off by diving into that gorgeous azure water and play with the porpoises. That was the tourist view.

But there was a darker, more sinister side to the land. Drugs, poverty, abuse, crime syndicates—each as dangerous as the piranha that infested the waters. People could disappear without a trace in Peru.

"Be careful, Samantha. Be very careful."

TWO

Forcing her eyelids apart, Samantha peeked out from under them and winced at the bright sunlight splashing on her face. She slipped her tongue over her dry, cracked lips, felt a hand slide under her neck.

"You are safe," a gentle voice murmured. "Sleep now."

When she woke up the second time, Sam was lying on a woven mat in some kind of hut made of huge leaves and poles. Her sandals sat against the wall. A girl appeared, touched her forehead and then smiled.

"Nonee," she said, pointing at herself.

"Hello, Nonee." Sam introduced herself. She followed the girl's bidding, sat up and chewed on the bit of breadlike food she was given while Nonee combed her hair, tenderly washed her face, then left. She returned with a big, burly man—like a teddy bear with a smile. He wore a crudely carved wooden cross on a leather cord around his neck.

"Hello."

She recognized the voice from earlier. "You're the padre Ramon told me about," Sam blurted out.

"Yes, I am the padre. Are you all right?" His concerned gaze took in her tattered clothes, her hair tumbling about her shoulders. "Nothing broken?"

Sam wiggled a bit, winced when her body protested. “Fine, I think. Just a little sore. I hit my head.” She was drawn in by his eyes—kind, gentle eyes that promised understanding. “I’m sorry if I gate-crashed your compound. I—I was running away.”

“There has been unrest in the jungle today. Things are not as they seem.”

“Then I should go.” She tried to get up and felt his big hand under her elbow, supporting her until she could stand on her own. “Thank you for helping me.”

“My dear, we are all God’s children. It is our duty to help one another.” Again he smiled and Sam could not look away from the peace she glimpsed in his face. She found herself longing to experience it personally.

A few moments later a gunshot broke the silence of the place. Birds squawked, children cried, a woman thrust her head into the hut and, in a frightened whisper, muttered, “*El Señor.*” The padre’s face tightened, but otherwise he gave nothing away, merely touched her hand to calm her and murmured a few indistinguishable words. Then he handed Sam her sandals.

“You are not safe here. Put on your shoes and then go with Nonee. Hide until I have dealt with this. Do not give yourself away. A man with evil in his heart is near. He will hurt you. Be very careful.” He touched her cheek then left.

Nonee bent and pointed to a small hole in the wall of the hut. Samantha began to crawl through the opening. At the last moment she saw her cell phone lying on the ground and snatched it up.

They emerged at the back of a group of huts, behind most of the furor. Nonee led the way upward, darting from dense thickets of eucalyptus trees through waist-high ferns, past huts where women ushered their little ones inside. Sam was so busy looking she almost bumped into Nonee, who had stopped abruptly and was now clearing away some limbs and debris from the base of a huge tree. After a moment a carved-out spot appeared in the trunk. This was the hiding place?

Nonee allowed no time for examination. She crawled in, and yanked on Samantha's hand for her to follow. Once they were both inside, she pulled back the branches and arranged them so that they had only the smallest peephole to see through.

Nonee looked through it just once. Apparently she didn't like what she saw, for she crossed her arms around herself and rocked back and forth, eyes closed, lips moving. At first Sam thought she was praying, until Nonee held out her palm, offering some of the raw white paste lying on it.

"*Bazuko,*" she offered, her voice hoarse. The word was familiar. A by-product of the cocaine-making process, *bazuko* was often used as a tranquilizer by the natives. Sam shook her head, turned back to watch.

Sounds from the camp were dimmer inside this secret cave. Voices raised loud in argument echoed toward them in fits and bursts. She could see two men standing on either side of the padre. They shook their fists, demanded something. The padre shook his head, and glared at a man dressed in tall boots and khakis who stood to one side. This was clearly the boss. Perhaps this was the el Zopilote she'd heard about.

Whoever he was, he said something Samantha couldn't hear. This time the priest waved his hand, encompassing the compound as he shook his head vehemently. El Zopilote or whatever his name was snapped out a command, ending the argument. Two men grabbed the padre and dragged him into the center of the camp where they bound him to a tree. The man she'd named el Zopilote stood with his back to Sam. In loud, clear Spanish he told the entire group that what had been stolen must be returned; he asked them to find it.

Furious and indignant, the padre insisted he leave, that they had nothing that belonged to him. The khaki man sneered, said something Sam didn't catch. Moments later the sound of a gunshot rang through the forest. The padre's head sank to his chest as the light in his eyes faded to nothing.

"No, oh no," she breathed, flinching but unable to tear her gaze from the horrible sight. When the murderer turned, she saw his face head-on, felt the pierce of his stare as if he could see through the trees and branches to the very spot where she hid. The evil in those eyes stabbed through her. Sam knew she'd never forget the feeling.

He gave an order and men began to tear the camp apart, obviously looking for something. They worked their way up the hill toward her, so close she could have reached out and touched them. Sam crawled backward until she bumped against something. In the gloom of her tree-cave her fingers trailed over the impediment, identified a chest of some sort. She leaned against it, held her breath as the footsteps came ever nearer. Nonee was shaking, sweating. Samantha wrapped an arm around her until the steps moved away.

After a few moments the dank smell of smoke permeated the air. Sam peeked out, surveyed the devastation. Many of the huts were burning as the natives stood watching, helpless against this onslaught. Children cried, women wept. The men held fisted hands at their sides.

El Zopilote said one word, then he and his men left. The sound of high-powered boat engines cut through the forest, silencing even the birds. In fact, everything seemed to go still as if mourning the loss of the kindly padre—until the drone of an airplane overhead brought awful reality back.

Sam would have moved then, but Nonee held her back and pointed. Outside Varga scanned the compound. Sam's fingers clenched into the dirt, startled at the cool press of metal against her palm. She glanced down, saw a small gold disk half-buried by the earth. As she turned to pick it up, she saw a second, then a third coin lying by the edge of the chest. It was too dark in the cave to examine them so she stuck them in her pocket. Nonee's hand grabbed her arm. Varga was moving toward them!

They pressed themselves against the back of the cave as a machete shoved through the branches and plunged into the ground in front of them. He grunted, removed the blade and moved on. A snake slid down a vine less than a foot in front of them, moved through the leaves and disappeared. Sam held her breath to stop the scream.

They waited for hours.

Finally Sam heard Varga's boat chugging back down the river. Through her peephole the compound looked deserted. Dusk dulled the atmosphere and smoke hung like wispy tapestries. El Padre lay where he had died. Though darkness was falling, no one lit a fire or set alight the torches. Murmurs and soft sobs filled the camp. It seemed the world was in mourning.

Nonee pointed to her sandals, made walking motions with her fingers. Sam nodded, glancing at the chest. Perhaps it had belonged to the padre, the treasure he couldn't take to heaven. Before she could look inside, Nonee's grip on her arm cut off all further thought as they slipped out of their hideaway.

Like thieves, they stole through the jungle, Nonee sure-footed as she found trails in the growing night. Weary, aching and heartsick, all Sam could do was keep following. Finally shards of light began to pierce the forest canopy. Nonee led the way onto a suspended bridge that spanned at least one-third of a mile and rose a hundred feet off the ground. Heights had never been Sam's forte, but going back wasn't an option. She gritted her teeth, looked straight ahead and tiptoed until she was sure the fragile construction would hold her weight. Connected by tree platforms, the bridge offered a spectacular view of the rain forest. Given other circumstances and more security, she might have admired the view. Today she could only think of the padre and the way his life had been snuffed out.

Like a band warming up, a cacophony of barbets, toucans and red-throated caracara joined the morning chorus of birdsong in swelling appreciation of dawn. The jungle steamed in reams of cloud upon *the eyelash of the forest,* as Peruvians termed it. Odors of decay and exotic floral perfumes mingled now, more pungent as heat mustered strength and crept up on the day. Drops of sweat pearled on Samantha's body, yet still they pushed on through the jungle.

She reckoned it was near midmorning before they emerged on a road, at the outskirts of a small settlement. Nonee motioned for her to stay, to wait.

"*Adios, mi amigo,*" Nonee whispered in halting Spanish, touching Sam's cheek with her fingertips. She smiled then she disappeared into the forest.

"Adios, chiquita. Muchas gracias."

Too tired to walk farther and with no idea which way to go, Samantha elected to wait. When she saw a bus trundling toward her, she reached into her pocket, hoping she'd find something to pay her fare. Her fingers closed around the coins and she drew them out to the light.

"Oh, my." Her hands shook so badly she could hardly turn them over to examine the other side. Not that she had to. She knew these coins as clearly as she knew her own name.

They were identical to the one Daniel wore around his neck on a thin gold chain. The coin he'd always refused to talk about.

Sam pocketed two of them, offered the third to pay her fare. The driver took it, put it between his teeth to check the gold consistency and finally nodded. She took a seat in the half-full bus and closed her eyes, reliving the past few hours as the vehicle bounced and jounced over the rough road.

Ramon, the poor, dead padre, these coins—whatever she'd stumbled into was about more than a statue gone missing. This was something darker, something more complex. She needed help. But if she asked, Daniel might take that as an admittance that she couldn't do her job.

They went through several small villages, dropping off or picking up passengers. At every stop Sam watched the driver speak to someone, show them the coin, jerk a thumb toward the bus. She knew he was talking about her but what could she do. She needed a ride.

The long, hot day stretched ahead. Sam laid her head back and shut her eyes as the bus bumped over potholes and stones. Sometime later she felt a hand on her arm and jerked awake. The burly driver told her she'd gone as far as the coin would take her, unless she had another. His suggestive look made her nervous. She shook her head. A moment later she was back on the road in a small peasant town and the bus was driving away.

Samantha started walking.

"It's been several days, Daniel. No contact with anyone—there or here. What could she be doing?"

He'd asked himself the same question a thousand times over and found no answer. It was pointless trying to fool Shelby that everything was all right. He couldn't even fool himself. "I don't know."

"There's a lot of unrest in Lima at the moment. Do you think we should send someone, maybe Callie Merton? Just in case Sam needs help."

"Callie's off on sick leave. She won't be back for several months." Privately, Daniel wasn't so sure Callie would ever be back. But that wasn't the point. If anyone went, it would be Daniel. He'd been the one to order Sam there; he'd be the one to bring her back. *Alive,* his brain screamed.

If I reported in every half hour, would that prove I know what I'm doing, Daniel? Is that what you make the other agents do, or is it only me? Because you don't trust me?

"If she's onto something I don't want to blow her cover too early." Or let her think I don't trust her. "Let's just wait a bit longer."

He stopped speaking when his secretary entered the office carrying a brown battered package addressed to him, marked personal and confidential. He raised one eyebrow, noted that security hadn't opened the tiny box.

"It's been scanned. Security says it's okay." Evelyn was good at reading his mind. "Can't read the postmark, but the initials are clear."

"From?" Shelby moved nearer.

"Samantha Henderson."

Daniel ripped it open. Inside he found a wad of newspaper and a small bag of coffee beans. He poured them onto his desk and stared.

"What is that?" Shelby stepped forward. "Daniel? Don't you have—"

"Yes." He lifted up a small golden coin, turned on a light and began to examine it under a magnifying glass. Using his fingernail, he scraped away a layer of sedimentary remains covering the gold. Identical.

"Is there a note?" Shelby rifled through the box and paper but found nothing. "What does it mean?" she asked.

"It means that Sam's on the trail of something." Daniel rose, holding the coin between his fingertips. "I'm not doing anything until tomorrow. If I don't hear from her at the appointed time, then we'll act."

Shelby left, grumbling about stubbornness. Daniel placed the coin under his microscope and studied it, compared it with the one he wore. He analyzed the two for a long time, barely noticed when his secretary left, when the whole floor went dark. Finally he leaned back, closed his eyes and whispered.

"Come on, Sam. Phone me!"

Daniel sat on, waited until security did their eleven-o'clock rounds, while the clock in the hall chimed midnight, still waited when the one-thirty red-eye to Seattle roared overhead.

He'd just closed his eyes to rest them when the phone rang.

He grabbed it, held it to his ear. "Sam?"

"Daniel?" The static covered most of her voice. "...coin. Something...wrong. No statue just.... Think—"

"Think what? Sam, are you in trouble?" A pause made the hairs on his arm rise. Why didn't she answer? "Do you need help?"

Static. Then one word penetrated.

"Yes."

"I sent her there, Shelby. I'll be the one who goes to find her."

"I thought you said Samantha was capable, that she knew her job."

"She does. But anyone can run into trouble." Daniel shook his head. "I know what you're thinking, Shel."

"Oh, what's that?" She sat watching him toss things into his briefcase.

"That I feel guilty or something for denying her that promotion. But you're wrong. This isn't personal."

"Isn't it?"

"Okay." He stopped fiddling and looked her straight in the eye. "We went out once. I thought it might go further but she didn't want that. Fine. But that had nothing to do with my decision not to promote her. There wasn't anything between us. Nothing serious."

She had that knowing look on her face. Daniel ignored it.

"We argued right before she left." It was more than an argument and he knew it. He bit his lip, admitted what Shelby already knew. "She's the only person around here who can make me say things I shouldn't. I let her go without straightening things out. I should have told her she merits promotion. It's just that I felt she needed more experience. Now she needs help and—"

"Daniel?"

"Yes?" He glanced up.

"Go."

"You really think—"

"*You* think—that's what is important here. Go to Peru or wherever she is. Find her." She rose, grinning. "You even have my blessing if that's what you want. Now what are you waiting for?"

"Nothing." He snapped the lid closed, swung the briefcase to his side and stepped around the desk. "I'll be back as soon as I can."

"Let me know if you need help and I'll send someone down. I'd prefer Callie, but—" She shrugged. "I'll find someone else if you need them."

He leaned over, hugged her and brushed a kiss against her cheek.

"My dear Shelby, did I ever tell you that the thing I like most about you is that you don't ask questions?"

She sniffed. "Not when I already know the answers. Be safe, Daniel."

He nodded and left, almost racing to the elevator. At the last moment before the doors closed, his secretary shoved a paper at him. Boarding at two in the afternoon. It was going to be tight, but he would be on that plane.

And he was.

As he pulled out his laptop and began to study the files he'd downloaded, Daniel was grateful he had the extra room first class provided. He began with the Finders file on the statue. Inca period. Held by a private collector for many years, the owner had a valuation certificate. He'd willed the statue to a museum in Brazil.

Two emissaries from a delivery service had picked it up for transport, but the statue had been stolen while in their possession. Finders job was to find the statue and get it to the museum.

The authenticity of that valuation certificate was still unverified and Tim's notes indicated he had questions regarding the theft. He used the onboard phone to call Shelby to see if there was any news.

"There was a message from Sam on the service telling you where to stay. She'll contact you."

He plugged the location into his laptop, grimaced at the hotel description. "This place looks pretty grungy. Couldn't Finders, Inc. spring for something a little more upscale?"

"Maybe she doesn't want to be noticed. You're too pampered, sitting in that office, rich boy."

Daniel detested being reminded of his father's wealth, money that was now his even if it was safely locked away in some bank gathering interest, and Shelby knew it. One of the reasons he stayed at Finders was that few people there knew or cared how much he was worth. They saw him as an ordinary guy, one of them. Well, everyone but Sam.

"Touché. I'm being a snob. I'll rough it." He looked at his notes. "Ask Tim to take another look at the pictures of the statue, will you?"

"Sure, but I should tell you he's more focused on the theft."

"Why?"

"He believes an art thief would have gone about things with more finesse. He's got someone checking with the police about it. I'll let you know."

"I'm sorry, Mr. McCullough." The attendant motioned to the tray and the phone. "We'll be landing in Lima in fifteen minutes. Please shut down your computer and end your call."

"Certainly." He nodded. "We're landing soon, Shel. I have to go."

"I'll keep digging. You find Sam."

"Count on it."

Daniel rubbed his fingers over the golden disk Samantha had sent. By the time he stepped onto Peruvian soil, the hairs on his neck were upright—never a good sign.

Evelyn had ordered a car to take him to the hotel. In his room, Daniel flopped across the bed to think. Like some people assembled a puzzle, his brain began to sort bits of information, trying to create order from chaos.

One problem ate at him. If the statue had been stolen for an art collector, why was it still floating around? The answer wasn't one he liked and once more warning signals went off.

Daniel sincerely hoped his instincts were wrong this time. Otherwise Sam was in deeper trouble than she knew.

THREE

"Don't say a word. Just get up and follow me."

Samantha waited for Daniel's nod of assent, then slid her fingers off his mouth. She handed him his glasses, watched him come fully awake.

"There are two men downstairs who will be here any minute, and they are not our friends. Hurry."

For once Daniel didn't argue with her. He slipped off the bed already clothed in jeans and a navy T-shirt. Either he'd been expecting her or he didn't trust the hotel's security. It took him twenty seconds to find his sneakers and pull them on. He grabbed his duffel bag and shoved his laptop and jacket inside it as the creak of a floorboard outside the door announced company.

"The fire escape." Samantha slid out the window opening and began climbing down the metal ladder, knowing he would follow if for no other reason than because he wanted answers. When she dropped to the ground, he was right behind her.

"Where now?"

At least he accepted that she was competent. Small comfort.

"For now just follow me. I'll explain later." Sam

pasted herself against the wall of the hotel then leaned forward to check the corner. A black car waited, engine running, which meant whoever was upstairs was prepared to follow her.

She pulled back to wait, held her finger over her lips when Daniel would have spoken. From above they heard voices. Confident they were almost invisible in the unlit alley, Sam glanced up and saw a head thrust through the window opening, scouring the street.

"Nobody here," someone said in Spanish. When a door slammed, she grabbed Daniel's hand.

"Run!"

She led him through a maze of streets and alleyways. Once, she heard a motor running and ducked into a doorway, pulling Daniel against her, praying his dark clothes would help hide them in the shadows. When the car slowed to take a second look and someone called out, she wrapped one hand around his neck and pressed her face into his chest, hoping her pursuers would ignore them. It worked.

"Sorry about that," she whispered when the car roared away, remembering only too well what it had felt like the first and only time Daniel had kissed her. "This isn't a very good section of town. They wouldn't be surprised to see a couple—er, carrying on."

"Not a problem." He stared at her, his amber gaze too shadowed to decipher. "What's next?"

"Ecuador." She moved quickly down the street.

Daniel jogged along beside her displaying not the least hint of weariness. Well, why would he? He'd been sleeping in a bed while she'd been trekking across half of South America.

She kept going, darting under gaily painted awnings,

checking corners before racing through streets that were just beginning to waken with the sun's first rays. When she thought they were free of their pursuers, she slowed to a walk. The back of her legs had begun to burn. Too much running lately.

"Any particular reason we have to go to Ecuador?" Daniel murmured, grasping her hand in his. "And what's with those clothes?"

She almost pulled away, until she noticed a police car rumbling toward them and decided to avoid questions by dragging him into a smelly, dirty side street.

"They're all I have, for the moment. Ecuador, because we're taking a cruise." She checked her watch. "We have a whole lot to do today if we're going to make our flight." Daniel looked like he was going to demand answers, but Sam ignored that. She knew what she was doing and if he didn't want to follow, that was up to him. Her muscles had uncramped enough for her to speed up her step and she did, knowing he'd keep up.

"I'm sure there's some very good reason we need to take a cruise at this particular point in time." His breath brushed against her earlobe.

"Of course." She glanced sideways.

"Because?"

"Because Varga and a well-known government official will be on the ship at noon tomorrow." She checked over one shoulder then urged him on.

"That's significant?"

Sam could hear the suspicion in his voice, as if he thought she was here holidaying.

"It is, because this official is the minister of antiquities."

"Ah. And you think—"

She sighed. "I don't know what to think anymore. All

I know is that Varga is taking the statue on that cruise and that somehow everything ties into this coin." She pulled it from her jeans pocket, stopping long enough for him to examine it.

"Another one? How many more have you got?" He held it beside the one she'd sent him and his own to see if it matched, then gave hers back.

Sam glanced around impatiently.

"Daniel, there's a lot to do. Yesterday I followed Varga to Torres Della Pina. He met some people there, apparently discussed selling something." She raised one eyebrow.

"I see. And Torres—?"

"It's a place where people, usually tourists, buy silver. I think he has or knows of more coins and wants to sell them. I'm assuming he met a buyer of precious metals at Torres. Maybe the statue is part of the deal." She shrugged. "He's going on that cruise and I'm going to follow him. I've got to put together some kind of disguise. So do you. That's your specialty, isn't it?"

He nodded. "But—"

"My info says he's headed to Ecuador—Quito, to be precise. It's half an hour from there to Guayaquil and another hour and a half to San Cristóbal, where we board the ship." She tapped her foot impatiently. "We can't afford to waste time. That is, if you're coming?"

"Of course I'm coming. That's why I'm here. But—"

"If you can just hold on to your questions for a while, I promise I'll get to them as soon as we've made passage. No!" She grabbed the arm he had almost raised to hail a cab.

"Wouldn't we get to wherever we're going more quickly in a cab?" he asked, his eyes on her hand circling his wrist. Sam immediately let go.

"In Lima it's not a good idea to hail a taxi in the street," she explained quietly. "Some of them are not what they seem and a lot are simply covers for hoods and thugs. Look for the official taxi stands." She pointed down the street. "Like that one. They are licensed by the city and are legit." She started walking and noted that he matched her step for step. "Don't get in it until we've settled on a fare. I don't know if you noticed but the taxis here don't use meters. It's better if you agree on a price first."

"I didn't know," he admitted. "Evelyn had a service pick me up at the airport. Thanks."

Well, at least he didn't hold it against her for knowing something he didn't. A wash of shame suffused her. Daniel wasn't the problem here. Sam vowed not to let their thorny past interfere with this job.

"We'll try this one," she decided, and began conversing with the taxi driver in Spanish. After several minutes she turned to Daniel and motioned for him to get inside. "Over there is the Miraflores area. I was tailing Varga there a few days ago in these same clothes, so I'd rather go elsewhere. Maybe we can shop in the San Isidro district. Then we'll head for Equador?"

"We?"

"I'm betting you didn't pack much in that duffel and we're going to need some dressy clothes on the ship."

"Won't showing up dressed to the nines draw more attention to us?" he asked when the driver had dropped them beside a sign that said Avenida Angamos.

"More like fit in. While you were flying down I had Finders do some background on cruises like this one. Our sailing involves a lot of very wealthy and important people, many known for their private collections—not acquired through any museum," she told him, lifting one eyebrow. "My point is that if they're on this cruise there has to be a reason. Maybe to bid on a statue?"

"Okay. So?"

"If we don't show up in something decent, we'll stand out like sore thumbs. We have to fit in as if we're as moneyed as the rest of them." She paid the driver and waited till he'd roared away. "You're the disguise master. Any suggestions?"

"You've never wanted to take the suggestions I made a few weeks ago, Sam. Why ask me now?" His eyes bored into her, demanded answers she didn't want to face.

"I only—"

"Only what? You told me you could manage anything Finders handed you. You accused me of misjudging you, of refusing to acknowledge your abilities. And a whole lot of other things." His amber eyes glittered hard, cold. "I'm only here because you said you needed help."

Meaning she'd proved she wasn't able to handle this case on her own. If only she'd never said it, never uttered those horrible, demeaning words. Sam had known they'd cut deep. She'd counted on hurting him as he'd hurt her. What she hadn't considered was that Daniel wouldn't forgive her.

"You're in charge here, Sam. What do *you* want to do?"

With a sigh she turned away.

"I don't know yet. But I'll figure something out," she mumbled tiredly. "I always do." She'd been running for so long. It would be wonderful to just let go and let him take over. But that would show her weakness, and Sam couldn't afford to let Daniel McCullough know she wasn't half as tough as she pretended to be.

Long, lean fingers closed around her arm, forcing her to turn and face Daniel.

"I'm sorry." He did look as if he regretted his words. "Let's agree to forget the past while we're here and concentrate on this job."

He'd made the first move toward a truce. Now, gentleman that he was, he would wait for her response.

"I'd appreciate any help you can offer," she whispered, trying to blink away the weak rush of tears that suddenly rose.

"Okay. I'll think about it while we're eating breakfast." He tilted her chin up, raised an eyebrow. "We do have time for breakfast?"

Sam checked her watch. "Yes. But what about you? Maybe we'd better come up with a disguise for you, too."

"I haven't run any missions in South America. It's unlikely I'd be recognized by anyone here, but I think I can remember past field experience long enough to come up with a few new looks, if necessary."

His attitude simmered with challenge. So the truce didn't include forgiveness. Samantha shrugged and chose to let it go. There was nothing to be gained by angering him. She chose a small café, ordered, then quietly ate her food. Daniel was apparently as deeply in thought as she. Finished, they left and walked up the street.

"Tell me more about this cruise."

"It's advertised as an anniversary/honeymoon cruise," Sam explained, deliberately avoiding his look. "All couples, no kids. That's a cover though. My information is that most of those registered were told there's something special planned. I think that's what drew them in the first place."

"Okay." He scratched his chin. "We'll get a list from Finders that will tell us who's on board and what they collect. Then we'll know which ones might be interested in the statue."

"I've already done that. Nothing jumped out, which only means they could be fake names." She chewed her bottom. "Intel says that cruises like these often have events planned—art sales or jewel displays, that kind of thing. If most of the guests on this one are wealthy, buying a few trinkets wouldn't be a problem for them."

"Trinkets?" Daniel made a face.

"Statues, maybe. Or coins." Samantha felt as if she were trying to persuade him to take a holiday. "Look, a pairs cruise isn't what I'd have chosen, but my orders are to find the statue. Varga is going to be on that ship, so I will be, too."

"Okay." He said nothing for a moment, then nodded. "We'll go on this cruise. Together."

"Fine." She waited for whatever he hadn't said.

"You realize we'll have to pose as a couple?"

Sam blinked, wondering why she hadn't expected that. Daniel ignored her to continue explaining his plan.

"We've got to fit in with the other guests—honeymoon and anniversaries, you said. We'll need clothing—spiffy, cruise wear. If we do it right, we'll simply look like any other pair enjoying the holiday. If we blend in we won't arouse suspicion while we're trying to get friendly with the others."

A couple? Them? Samantha sent him a look that would have quelled lesser men. Daniel smiled, but there was a set to his mouth that told her he'd already decided their next course of action.

"Stop looking at me like that. We both know it isn't true, so what's the harm. If Varga's there with the statue, we'll look like any other buyer."

He was taking over again, pulling rank. Sam bit her lip to stem her frustration.

"Which brings us back to disguises," he said, studying her disheveled look.

"I've been tailing Varga, but I'm not sure he could identify me up close."

"He's certainly been globe-trotting." Daniel rubbed his shadowed chin. "Any thoughts why he would have led such a merry chase?"

Samantha had asked herself the same question and hadn't found a satisfactory answer. "I assumed he was trying to find a dealer."

"One that lives up the Amazon?" Daniel raised an eyebrow. "And if that's the case, why does Varga still have it? Why take the statue on a cruise? Tim's got some questions he's checking into, too."

"You want to call the whole thing off?" Sam pretended disinterest. "Wait till you can verify things at Finders?"

"I assumed we had. Now I'm not sure something wasn't fudged." Daniel's amber eyes narrowed as he studied her, then he shook his head. "No, if we're wrong and we lose him now, our client loses. We'll go on the cruise, learn what we can." He passed his hand down the swath of hair that fell past her shoulders, almost to her waist. After a few moments he drew his hand away. "It's rather like a shield, isn't it?"

He sounded so strange, almost sad. What was wrong with him? Sam counted to ten then cleared her voice. "Daniel? Disguises?"

"That's what I was talking about. This—" he plucked a handful of hair and raised it "—is your trademark. I'm sure Varga made you, but I doubt he's ever seen past it."

"So?" A pained look washed through his eyes. Sam flinched under the intense scrutiny. "What?"

"I hate this idea more than you know, Samantha, but my suggestion is to cut your hair."

"Huh?"

"It's one of your best features, but also your most noticeable. If you were to cut it short, maybe add some curls or tint it a different shade it's doubtful anyone would recognize you. Your hair is beautiful, Sam, but you do tend to hide behind it." He waited for a response. "Well? Have you got a better idea?"

At the moment she hadn't. Samantha stopped in front of a store window and studied herself. She'd let her hair grow for so long it had become second nature. But that didn't mean she was hiding from anything. She didn't have to hide. *She'd* been honest and upfront about her intention to do the job.

Still, the idea had merit. She told him she was going to be a while, walked into the nearest salon and made her request. She walked out an hour later with a cap of feathery curls that made her feel about six years old, ten pounds lighter—and maybe just a little vulnerable.

Daniel was pacing in front of the salon. She walked up behind him and touched his arm. "Is this what you meant?"

"Excuse me, I—" He blinked, took a second look. "Wow! Even I didn't recognize you for a minute." Daniel walked around her, his lips pursed. "You're still beautiful, Samantha, but the hair makes you look young and chic, sort of cover-girlish." He shook his head. "I'm expressing this badly."

"You're doing all right," she murmured, embarrassed by his approval and the odd tone of his voice. Desperate to get his attention off her, she pointed. "Let's try that store for clothes. I'm afraid I lost most of my stuff on the Amazon. We'll have to keep an eye on the time though."

"I'd like to hear about that, but I suppose it will have to wait until later."

They began the search for suitable cruise clothes. To her surprise, Daniel vetoed a couple of items she selected, chose other things—dresses she'd never dream of wearing. Since her job had always entailed clothes that never stood out, and since Daniel wore custom suits to work, she decided to trust his judgment, though parading in front of him dressed to the nines made her uncomfortable.

"It looks fantastic on you, darling," he crooned while the salesperson hovered, a fawning smile on his face. "You might as well get the sun hat, as well. We don't want that delicate skin aging too early."

Even though she knew the hat could be useful, the low rumble of his voice, that gentle note of pretend caring sent Samantha's defenses up. If this was his idea of couplehood, he was in for trouble.

"Honey," she responded, gripping his forearm, "I'll be fine. But what about you? I can see a tinge of red on your neck already."

What she'd expected, Samantha wasn't sure, but it didn't include him prying her fingers off and wrapping them in his own as he leaned forward to whisper just loud enough for the staff to hear, "You can smooth some lotion on it for me later, darling."

She gave him a scathing look meant to diminish the twinkle in his eyes. He ignored it and bent to murmur in her ear.

"Dinner is a big deal on board. You'll need something special for at least three evenings."

Sam adjusted her perspective. "You've been on a cruise before."

"There are lots of things you don't know about me, Samantha," he said, his tone brimming with insinuation.

Daniel insisted on buying three gorgeous dinner gowns. Sam pretended nonchalance. She could hardly tell him that the thought of wearing those silken delights made her mouth water. Why hadn't she ever been given a dress-up assignment before?

"We're only allowed one suitcase on the flight and that can't weigh more than forty-four kilos," she reminded him while the pile of to-be-bought grew. "Besides, the cruise has a lot of walking and exploring."

"Some shorts and shirts, jeans, then we'll be finished," he promised.

His proprietorial air was beginning to get to her. "Why don't you just go ahead and choose my wardrobe, honey?" she offered sweetly, wishing she'd never made that call for help to Finders. "I'll sit here and wait for you." She should have known it wouldn't quell him.

"Good idea." Daniel smiled but continued handing over articles to the beaming saleswoman.

Samantha tried to ignore his dangerously attractive grin and focus on the job. A newspaper lay on a table beside her very plush chair. Varga had studied Lima's newspaper on three occasions when she'd been tailing him.

She scanned the newsprint and had almost given up when she saw it—an exhibit of Inca treasures would be displayed aboard a cruise ship to the Galapagos Islands. So that was the drawing card. As she removed the section from the newspaper, she noticed a man leaning against a pillar near the store's entry, a man she'd seen before.

Stifling her panic, Samantha slowly rose, sauntered over to Daniel, who had moved his attention to the men's department and was amassing a collection for himself.

Sam slid her arm through his and rose on tiptoe to whisper in his ear. "Daniel, there's a man outside that was with Varga on the river. If he recognizes us he's going to make it difficult to get to the airport."

There was one thing Samantha had always admired about Daniel McCullough. He didn't bother asking a lot of silly questions. Once apprised of a situation he took immediate action. "Change into the white slacks and the yellow top," he murmured. "That hat should come in handy now."

After a discussion with the salesman, the clothes were paid for and bagged. A few moments later they strolled out the door, Sam's huge red hat hiding her face.

"He didn't seem to know you." Daniel's grin was contagious.

"That's the idea." The way the silk top grazed her skin made Sam feel distinctly uncomfortable. The way Daniel was watching her added to her unease. "We need some suitcases. That beaded gown weighs a ton."

"Yes, it does. But I can bear up under the strain imagining you in it." He chuckled at her glower, motioned to the shop window. "How about those cases to put them in?" With little fuss Daniel purchased two bags, slipped their things inside. Moments later they were outside on the street. "Now what?"

"Our tail is back." Sam noted Varga's friend talking on a pay phone. Daniel followed her inside a small drugstore to watch. A black car slid up to the curb and waited. It looked like the one from Daniel's hotel. Varga arrived moments later and spoke to the other man.

"Watch them for a minute, will you?" She grabbed a few necessities, paid for them, then returned.

"That was quick." Daniel turned from his study out the window, took her sack and slid it inside the suitcase.

"Some things don't take much thought. Varga left in the car?"

He nodded but said nothing, merely followed her out the door. She turned and scanned the street.

"Nobody's watching," he murmured. "I already checked."

"Me, too." She didn't tell him that she couldn't help checking, especially after her experience in the jungle.

"Relax, Sam." Daniel's hand brushed hers. "He's busy with his own plans. You're certain he's heading for the cruise ship, right?"

"That's my information."

"If we've time before we catch the plane, I wouldn't mind stopping for a drink while you get me up to speed. I'm not used to this heat."

She nodded. The time for managing on her own had passed. She'd asked for help, now she'd share what she knew. A nearby sidewalk café was only half filled. Sam chose a table where she could keep an eye on whoever passed. Daniel set the bags by her feet and pulled out his phone.

"I'll be over there. I'm going to check in with the office." He moved away.

"Inca Kola." The boyish waiter grinned at her choice of a favorite Peruvian drink. Daniel was still on the phone when the boy brought her the fizzy soft drink. She took a sip, let the cream-soda flavor mixed with a hint of bubble gum soothe her dry throat. She did a second check of the area. Nothing.

"What is that you're drinking?" Daniel asked.

Samantha gaped, amazed by the simple change he'd made to his appearance. Suddenly he looked like a rich playboy. "Where are your glasses?"

"In my pocket." He sat down and took a sip of her drink. "What is that?"

She explained, smiling at his grimace. "Don't worry. I'll order you something you will like." She waved over the waiter. "Chicha morada."

"Should I be worried?" he asked, when a rich deep purple drink was set before him.

"No. It's an old Inca drink made from purple corn infused in water with pineapples, sugar, lemon juice and cinnamon served over ice. It's supposed to be very refreshing."

"Then why aren't you drinking it?" he demanded.

"Allergy. I have two of them. Any kind of seafood and cinnamon."

"Ah, Samantha Henderson has a weakness." He frowned suddenly as he grabbed her arm. "What's this from?" One thumb gently brushed the damaged skin on her wrist.

"All part and parcel of the job working for Finders, Inc." She pulled, but Daniel wouldn't let go.

"You're hands are raw!" he exclaimed. "Your nails look like you scrabbled your way up a mountain."

"Close, boss."

"Stop calling me that!" he hissed. "I came here to try and help you. Maybe it's time you told me why you asked me to come."

"I didn't ask you to come." Samantha flushed under his scrutiny. "Not exactly. I said I needed help."

"There's a difference?"

"Yes." Why did she always feel she had to prove herself to him? Samantha suppressed the irritation he brought out in her, and began her story anew. Better to tell him and get it over with.

"I stumbled onto something. Literally and figuratively. I don't know what it means except that I think the statue I'm tracking has something to do with those coins I found. Since you already have one, I thought maybe you could explain where it came from."

He fingered the small gold disk that lay against his chest. "I've had this for a very long time, Sam. I don't think it could tie into anything you got mixed up in."

"But it has to! It's exactly the same. You examined the one I sent you, didn't you?" she demanded when it seemed he'd deny her conclusion. "Is there any difference?"

"No." He pursed his lips. "Tell me where you found it."

"I was tracking Varga." She closed her eyes and launched into her story. When she got to Ramon she had to stop.

"You got off the boat?" he fumed, interrupting her midsentence. "You realize he could have left you there? You should have stuck with him." Daniel's eyes blazed.

"If I had I'd be dead, just like Ramon." Sam met his glare. "I found him floating facedown in the water with a knife sticking out of his back."

Daniel looked chastened. "I did it again, didn't I? Jumped to conclusions. I promise to shut up while you tell me the rest."

She stared at the glass in her hand, absently noticing the collection of condensation drops on its outside, just like the leaves in the jungle after a rain.

"Go on, Sam."

"I fell, hit my head, blacked out. When I woke up I

was in some kind of hut. A kind, gentle man, the padre, helped me. Then things got crazy." She closed her eyes, not wanting him to see the terror that still haunted her. "I was hiding and saw him arrive."

"Varga?"

"Later, yes. But another man came first. I'm assuming he was el Zopilote. He was furious, kept asking the padre to return what had been stolen. The padre kept denying he had whatever it was." She paused, swallowed. "Men began searching the camp. I didn't really feel threatened until Varga started sticking his machete into things."

"So this el Zopilote wasn't tracking you?"

"I don't think so." She closed her eyes and relived those moments. "They tore things apart, small, large. It didn't seem to matter. What they didn't tear they burned."

"So they found what they wanted?"

"No. I don't think so."

"You were hiding—by yourself?"

"Not exactly. I had a friend." She couldn't tell him about the shooting. It was too new, too profound. To see the padre's kindly light, that gentle spirit extinguished—how could she forget that?

"Sam?" Daniel's quiet question drew her back to the present, to the job she'd been sent to do.

"I'm fine." She gathered her composure. "We waited till it was over, then my friend got me through the jungle to a dirt road." She explained about the bus.

"Did the driver say why you had to get off?"

"He wanted another coin. I refused and started walking. A nice farmer gave me a ride to Iquitos. A friend picked me up there. When I got back to Lima, I went to the bank, mentioned Finders—you know the drill." He nodded. "I took a shower, slept then checked out a couple of Varga's haunts and learned his friends were asking questions about me all over town."

"The same friends you saw on the boat."

"Yes. Except for el Zopilote. I haven't seen him since the jungle." Fear crawled up her back remembering the icy cold hate on his face. "After we heard the plane I never saw him again."

"An airplane?" Daniel's whole body went still as he searched her face. "You're saying the padre had an airplane?"

"El Padre Dulce is what Ramon called him. I don't know the plane was his, though. They killed him, destroyed everything, and they all took off. I heard a boat and a plane." Something was going on with Daniel. His whole body had gone on high alert. His face was whiter than snow and his fists curled at his sides. "What's wrong?"

"I'm not sure. You said these people killed el Padre Dulce?" She nodded. "I need to make another call. It could be a long one."

"You'll have to make it in the cab," Sam told him, shocked by the time. "We need to get going. Now." She bartered with a taxi driver who agreed to take them to the airport. During the long ride, Daniel tried his phone without success. Eventually he put it away and sat silent, seemingly lost on some unseen private vista. A little muscle at the corner of his jaw ticked, proof that something was not right.

At the airport Sam repacked their cases to prevent questions. They purchased their tickets, went through security and waited for boarding. At last Sam relaxed, fairly certain that no one could get to them in the holding lounge.

Daniel did not relax.

"I'll be over there. My cell's not working and I need to call Evelyn." He jiggled it then headed for the pay phones on the wall.

Sam pulled out her own phone which seemed to be working once more. She text-messaged the office to ask for an updated client manifest from the cruise ship. Finders messaged back a string of names. One name in particular held her attention. She already knew the Peruvian minister of antiquities would be sailing with them, but now the list included another man—a museum curator who also collected Inca artifacts.

Daniel returned and flopped down in the seat beside her. She began to tell him what she'd found, then realized he wasn't paying any attention to her. His eyes were frozen on the wall opposite them, his face shuttered, closed in. Something was very wrong.

Sam studied the downward slope of his shoulders, the way he rubbed his temple. He'd put his glasses back on but his eyes were closed and his lips were moving. He was praying.

A shudder of trepidation skittered over her skin.

The trouble hadn't originated from Finders, Inc. or they'd have let her know. So it was something else. Something he wasn't telling her.

Yet.

Day turned to night during their flight to Quito. Daniel couldn't rest. Evelyn, of course, was visiting her granddaughter. Since he had no intention of spoiling her evening, he tried Shelby but found her unavailable.

That ought to tell him something. If there had been an incident, if anything had happened—no! He closed his eyes and whispered another prayer, imploring God to do what he couldn't. But deep in his heart he knew.

In Quito, morning rush hour raged. By the time they left the terminal, finding a train to Guayaquil proved difficult. When they finally alighted dockside to wait for their cruise from San Cristóbal, Daniel was tired, and more tense than the day Shelby had gone into labor at the office.

"It's after eight Victoria time. The office should be open. I'm going to try Finders again."

"Now you know why I didn't call in very much. Sometimes getting through isn't as easy as it should be."

"Apparently. All I got on the pay phones was a busy signal."

"Is your phone working again?"

He pulled it out, checked. "Looks like it. Maybe there was a short or something." There were two messages. The first was from Shelby. He took a deep breath as he punched the button.

"I'm sorry to tell you this way, Daniel, but a message arrived here today from a mission society notifying you of your uncle's death, Bert McCullough. Here's a number you can call for more information. Call me whenever you want. I'm so sorry, Daniel."

It took several moments for the words he'd dreaded to sink in. Uncle Bert—gone. It seemed impossible. Daniel had seen him last Christmas and Bert had been fine. A little thin, perhaps, but then with his work—

"Daniel, it's Tim. I can tell you that the police think the robbery was planned and carried out by someone with intimate knowledge of the route and the security involved. The shipper's office in Rio reported a break-in. The statue was the only package stolen. Today I spoke to the former owner's sons, who recalled that a man visited their father the night he died. This fellow took a lot of pictures of the statue, asked when it would be shipped, etc. Looks like it was planned from the get-go. Just thought you should know. Talk to you later."

"What's wrong?" Sam frowned as he closed the phone, her face showing her worry. "What happened?"

"My uncle died." It burned his throat to say it. "Uncle Bert. He was the one who raised me after my father died." He swallowed the rest, unwilling to voice his suspicions. Not now and not here. First he needed time and space to accept it.

"I'm very sorry, Daniel." Her warm hand covered his and he clutched it like a lifeline.

"So am I." He found himself craving her touch and longed to pull her close and believe, just for a moment, that she cared. Maybe because he couldn't do that, his lips wouldn't stop blabbering. "Bert was a wonderful man. The least selfish person you could ever hope to find. Every summer he'd take some time off just so we could be together." He gulped. "He was the most loving man I knew."

In silence she shared his grief. Then her voice entered his consciousness. "They've finally begun boarding."

He didn't know how much time had passed before she said that. He stared at her stupidly, surprised she hadn't moved from his side.

"Would you rather call this whole thing off, Daniel?"

"Call it off?" He shook his head and gritted his teeth together. "No. Bert's gone. There's nothing I can do for him. Let's go."

"If you change your mind, let me know."

Passengers anxious to board made staying in line a

challenge. He stood behind Sam, shielding her as he stared down at her short curls glossy in the bright lights. They'd been ushered through the main gate with no problem, proof that she'd planned ahead, but security came back to check that their yellow fever vaccinations were up to date. After several flirting remarks, the guy moved on. Daniel gave him the once-over, memorized his face.

"Tell me again why we're going on this cruise?" he asked as the line stalled again. *Say anything that will help me think of something else.*

"That's right, I didn't have time to tell you." She pulled a paper out of her pocket and handed it to him. "That was in the newspaper. I also don't think it's a coincidence that the Minister of Peruvian Antiquities is sailing on this cruise." She showed him the list of names. "I've run into Obrigado a couple of times. He's a shady character, circumvents normal customs procedures for his friends."

"A gold display. The security for that must be a nightmare." He fingered the coin at his neck. "But the statue isn't gold. Do you really think Varga's going to make the transfer during the cruise?"

"That's my information and the day I arrived back in Lima, it was confirmed." Tired of holding her big red hat, she set it on her suitcase. "I have several questions whose answers elude me. I followed Varga for ages, and he never seemed to notice me or care that I was there if he did. But suddenly I'm back in Lima and he and his goons were combing the city for me. It doesn't make sense."

"Nor does bringing the statue here. He'd have to smuggle it aboard, and with all this security I can't see how." Daniel knew his skepticism showed.

"Maybe in that gold display?" Her nose wrinkled as it

always did when she brainstormed scenarios. "Obrigado could claim he purchased it on the ship and that would get it back to Peru—no, that's silly. It was already *in* Peru." She stepped forward, handing the official her documents and their tickets. Daniel also held out his passport.

"Mr. McCullough, you and the lovely *señorita* have a suite on the Solana deck. Your bags will be delivered to your room. Enjoy your cruise."

"Thank you."

Sam swung her hat at her side as she led the way up the stairs and across the boarding section. Offered such a view, Daniel couldn't help admiring her trim figure in the white slacks and bright yellow top. She certainly looked the part of a wealthy tourist. Elegant and poised, her darkened skin only added to her beauty. She grasped his hand once they were on deck, her smile wide and engaging.

"I've never been on a cruise before, Daniel. It should be interesting. You were in Special Ops with Grant, so I guess you don't get seasick."

Daniel thought of the past and almost scoffed at the suggestion. A second later he wondered how she'd known he was in Special Ops. She'd mentioned his past before, too. He'd have to ask her about that later.

A steward directed them to the glass elevators, which she stepped into gingerly, her fingers tightening around his.

"Sorry," she whispered. "I don't like heights. I don't know how I ever made it across a suspension bridge in the jungle."

"Necessity is a great motivator." Mindful of the others crowding in around them, Daniel took the opportunity to slide his arm around her waist and draw her against him, hoping she'd remember his idea to pretend to be a couple. He'd have to remind himself it was all pretend, too.

Sam twisted her head, gave him a look, but the elevator was too full for her to move any distance away. Daniel leaned his chin against the top of her head and tried to hide his smile of satisfaction. Foolish maybe, but he'd dreamed about this once. Before he'd ruined everything.

They arrived at the appropriate deck. Free of the elevator, Sam scooted away from him as if she'd been burned, charging ahead toward the suite she'd reserved. Their suitcases were waiting at their door and he carried them inside without looking at her.

"I figured I'd only get to do this once so I got us a balcony suite. I hope you don't mind. Finders can dock my pay if you want. It will be worth it." Her words came a little too quickly.

She was nervous. Daniel watched her walk across the thick broadloom and drag open the patio door. One whiff of the pungent diesel aroma had her sliding it closed faster than she'd opened it. "Maybe we'll wait on breathing the healthy seaside air."

"Sam." He stood watching her, wishing now that he'd kept his distance. They had to work together and that relationship was his top priority right now. It had to be.

"Oh, look. There's a fruit basket. Lovely. I'm starved, aren't you? The papaya looks perfect."

Daniel told himself to wait, but he lost his cool when she pulled off her scarf, swung around, and he saw her neck. There were marks there, too.

"Sam."

"Yes?" She frowned at him.

"I need to get something straight. Varga was at the camp with the other man or he came later?"

She closed her eyes for a moment, thought it out. "I don't think he was there at first, even though I saw his boat just before I fell. In fact, things had died down a bit before he showed up. Him and his two goons."

"How would he have known you were there? You said you were following him, not the other way around."

"It has recently occurred to me that he was luring me there. You had to hear that boat to understand—fast, slow, fast, slow. Never out of sight." She thought a moment. "Also I left my backpack in the boat with Ramon, but when I saw Ramon's boat beside Varga's, the packages and my pack were missing." She explained about Ramon's cargo. "If Varga looked in the backpack, he had to know I was somewhere around."

"But why kill Ramon?" Something wasn't right about this. Daniel set it aside while he heard the rest. "The other guy—el Zopilote? That can't be his only name."

"I don't know any more about him," Sam admitted. "I don't think I want to. He looked evil."

"It could be important for us to know who we're dealing with."

"I know. I asked Finders about el Zopilote but they had nothing. I guess I assumed the guy was Varga's boss, that they were both after me." She shook her head, her eyes troubled. "The thing is Varga has no history of violence."

"Yet. So he led you to this cruise and that's why I'm here?" Not that he needed to be anywhere else. The time for helping Bert had gone.

"Him and a few tips. Everything I've found leads here. The only explanation is that Varga must be getting rid of the statue. Finally." Sam gnawed on her bottom lip. He was here, why not use him as a sounding board. "Daniel, did you read the report on the theft of that statue?"

"Tim apprised me of his concerns."

"Good. Then you know it wasn't a random theft. The statue was carefully chosen." She waited for his nod. "Why steal it if there wasn't already a buyer who had the money? Why cart it all over the place if it's valuable?"

"Crime of opportunity? He heard about it, wanted to see if he could get his hands on it?"

She shook her head. "As far as I could find out, Varga hasn't been off the continent recently. I think someone else stole the statue, passed it to him."

"Maybe the statue is a fake?"

"Why would Varga bother with a fake? It's a lot of work for a scam and people who pay big money for art don't like to be scammed, so he'd make some nasty enemies." She chose a peach from the fruit bowl and bit into it. "These are good. Try one."

"Maybe later." He closed his eyes as he rubbed the bridge of his nose. "Could there be something intrinsically valuable about the statue itself?"

"Other than that it's probably Inca in origin?" Juice dribbled down her chin and she grabbed a napkin and dabbed it away. "I don't think so."

"Try another angle. Maybe it isn't about the statue."

"What then?" She peered at him. "You're getting at something and I don't understand what. Ever since you took that message you've closed in on yourself. What's wrong?"

Truth time. Pain shot through his heart. Daniel grabbed a bottle of water and took a drink.

"The padre you saw in the jungle, el Padre Dulce you called him."

"Yes?" She raised one eyebrow. "What about him?"

"I think he was my uncle." Daniel hated seeing the sheer horror fill her face, but he had to say it.

"Samantha, I think you watched someone kill my uncle Bert."

FOUR

"What!" Samantha's face drained of color.

"I suspected something as soon as I heard you say *Dulce.* My uncle Bert is—was a priest. He's had a mission in the jungle for years. *Dulce* was a nickname he got long ago. It had to be him you saw being shot."

One hand covered her mouth, her green eyes brimming with tears. "I wish I could have stopped it."

"So do I, Samantha, believe me." He sat down in one of the armchairs rubbing his temple to ease the throb. Sam tossed the peach pit into the garbage. She walked to the bathroom to wash her hands and returned, drying them on a white towel. "I need to be sure. Can you tell me anything about the compound you were in?"

"It had a flag flying. An unusual-looking cross on a white background."

"The mission flag." Daniel's heart sank lower as any possible doubts melted. "Describe the man you saw killed. What did he look like?"

She stared at him for a moment, then spoke, wiping her fingers as she told him—probably so she wouldn't have to look at him. "I didn't really see him for very long. What I really noticed were his eyes." A tear slid down her cheek and dangled on her chin. “He had such compassionate eyes.”

“Eyes the same color as mine?”

“Yes.” She peered into them. “I don’t know why I didn’t connect that.”

Daniel kept a rigid control on his emotions as the details fell into place. “Six one or two with balding head, big biceps, a wooden cross on a leather strip around his neck.”

Her eyes grew round and wide. “Yes,” she whispered.

“Uncle Bert was a missionary in the jungle for thirty years. I should have connected it sooner but I thought he was on leave. He was supposed to be having some medical tests done in the States. He probably put them off. He never acknowledged ill health.” A faint smile rose at the memory. “Bert always said the Quechuans could come up with a medicine for anything he caught. He loved them like family.”

“Quechuan?” She stumbled over the word, her voice soft in the room.

“A tribe in the Andes, near the mouth of the Amazon. My uncle worked with them on and off for years. Actually he spent his first term as a missionary with them.”

“So el Zopilote murdered a missionary.” The wretched words seemed dragged from her. “I wish I’d never gone there.”

“I’m glad you met him, if only for a little while. He was a very special man.” Daniel closed his eyes, trying to recall that last letter. “He mentioned some problems he’d been having in his compound. Something about a plane. He said we’d talk about it next time we got together. Now I wish I’d asked some questions.”

“He was an actual priest?”

Daniel nodded. "'Father Bert' the kids in Lima called him. 'El Padre Dulce' was a silly kind of nickname they gave him because he loved to suck on lemon drops. The title stuck. He was the exact opposite of my father in every way, yet the two were quite close. I never understood that."

"I'm so sorry." Sam collapsed onto the sofa, her whole body drooping. "I don't know what else to say to you. You probably think I should have tried harder to help him. I wish I had. If I'd known what would happen I'd have done anything to stop them from shooting him."

Daniel walked toward her then hunkered down in front. "Don't dwell on it, Sam. Uncle Bert was ready to give up his life at any time, he was prepared to die. He always said God would look after him until it was time to go home." He clasped her hands in his, squeezed them, then reached up to brush away a tear that bloomed on her cheek. "I'll miss him, but it wasn't your fault."

"But why did they kill him? That's what I don't understand. Why?"

"There was an argument you said. Maybe they wanted more of those coins you found?" He rose and turned away from her so that Sam wouldn't read the struggle he was certain was visible on his face. He hated the past, hated discussing it, hated even thinking about it. But maybe the past was the only way to explain what they needed to know.

"No, I don't think so. The padre said he didn't have whatever they were looking for." Sam stared at his throat. "Where did it come from Daniel?"

He picked up his coin, rubbed his thumb over it. "It was so long ago."

Sam touched his arm. She snuggled against his side as if to impart some comfort. "Tell me."

Glad of her nearness, he wrapped an arm around her waist, took a deep breath and let the story pour out of him.

"My father was consumed by business, by making more money. I barely saw him when I was growing up. He went in to work early and he came home late."

"Your mother?" Her voice was muffled against his shirt.

"She died just after my third birthday. I don't remember her very much." He threaded his fingertips through the silky curls, wishing he could avoid this. "Anyway, Dad always thought I'd follow him. He was constantly trying to groom me for his job and, as I got older, he got more intense about it. That's where Uncle Bert came in. Every so often he'd wire Dad a note saying he had a week or two off and wanted to see us. We'd fly down the coast to Lima, Bert's headquarters, and Uncle Bert would show us the sights. I was about eight when Dad first heard the story of the *Isadora*."

"The what?" She blinked up at him, her eyes wide.

"It's the name of a Spanish galleon that sailed these waters in the 1700s. Supposedly it sank with a load of gold on board. After he heard about it, Dad decided we'd rent a boat and try to find the buried treasure."

Holding her was too easy. He needed to face these ghosts on his own. Daniel dropped his arms, stepped back and took a seat on a nearby easy chair.

"That began our quest. Every summer, for eight blessed, wonderful weeks I was free of the constant pressure and nagging. I slept on deck, watched the stars come out and ate fish by the gallon."

"So you beat seasickness young."

"I've always loved the water. Dad and Bert were born near the ocean and had both learned to scuba years before.

Bert taught me when I was nine. Each day we'd dive in the ocean, looking for buried treasure." He half smiled at her bemused look. "A treasure hunt—it was a boy's dream come true. One person would remain on deck while the other two went down, searching for the ship."

"Every summer for how long?" Sam sank onto the carpet at his feet, her green eyes snagging diamonds of light and reflecting them back as she leaned forward to listen.

"Until I was sixteen. We'd made good progress that year, found a lot of things that told us the *Isadora* was nearby. We hadn't found the gold, but my father was certain we would. It was merely a matter of time." He smiled, remembering how he'd thought that perfect time would never end. "I didn't care if we never found it. I was addicted to diving by then, just as they were."

"I never knew that."

"Why would you?" He hadn't meant it as a challenge, but Samantha had never seen him as anything other than her boss and that was something he wished he could change.

He mocked himself for not accepting that the feelings had been all on his side, that she simply didn't see him as someone she could trust.

"Go on with your story, Daniel. I'm listening."

"Okay." He took a deep breath. "One morning Uncle Bert decided to dive early, probably because my father was riding me about some formula for gauging foreign interest bond profits and I lipped off. Uncle Bert was good at stepping between us."

"But surely he wouldn't dive alone?"

"No, that was our unbreakable rule. Always dive with a buddy. So I went with him." Daniel swallowed, hard. "My dad asked me to carry up a chest from below before I went, but I deliberately ignored him. I was sick of his orders, of his harping, of business. I just wanted to get away. Uncle Bert didn't like my attitude, but he made it a point to stay out of our arguments."

"So you dived with him." She leaned forward, eyes wide with childlike expectancy.

"Yes. I was just playing really, paddling along with the fish. A minute later I saw gold coins scattered all over the ocean floor, just waiting to be picked up. I grabbed one, took it to my uncle to show him. Once he got over his excitement, he waved me up and we both began to surface."

"Why? I would have been stuffing my pockets."

Daniel smiled at her enthusiasm. "No pockets on a wet suit. We needed to get pails, a marker, something. And I think my uncle wanted to make a notation of the exact spot in case the wind shifted or something. Anyway, up we went." He rubbed a hand over his face then forced the words out. "We found my father below decks, the trunk on the floor beside him. He'd suffered a massive heart attack trying to carry it upstairs. We headed for port as fast as we could, but there was nothing they could do. He'd been alone too long."

"It wasn't your fault," she declared staunchly.

"Wasn't it, Sam?" Even now the guilt ate at him. "I knew he wasn't well. If I'd moved the trunk before I went down it would never have happened. But I got so focused on finding the treasure—" He shook his head, pulled out the chain around his neck. "This coin is a reminder not to get so tied up in myself that I forget about others."

As he fingered the disk, Daniel realized it hadn't

helped. He'd taken for granted that Bert would always be there, that when he had time he'd see his uncle again, listen to his problems and maybe lend a hand. Now it was too late. Same old lesson repeating itself.

Samantha was silent for a long time. Before she could speak, the horn sounded, the ship got under way. They went topside to watch the departure, neither saying much as the dock grew smaller. Some time later everyone was ordered to practice for a fire drill. Daniel followed Sam to the appropriate deck and went through the motions. While they listened to instructions he scanned the faces of his fellow passengers. None of them looked familiar.

"So far no one is following us and, anyway, there's nowhere to run on this ship. Let's get something to drink and sit in the sun," Sam urged once the drill was complete. She drew him toward a small drink bar near the rear of the ship. "I'll snag some chairs, you get the drinks. Something sweet and fizzy for me, please."

He carried the tall frosted glasses to the back deck where Sam lay sprawled in a recliner, staring at the receding vista of San Cristóbal. She took a greedy gulp of her drink, motioned for him to sit next to her.

"I don't understand how what happened to you at sixteen ties into my finding the coin in the jungle."

"Uncle Bert never stopped looking for that treasure," he told her, careful to keep his voice quiet. "I went down with him a couple of times over the years, just for fun. Uncle Bert took it more seriously. Obviously he found the coins."

"If the entire trunk was full, they must be worth a fortune," she mused, her gaze on the receding horizon.

"Trunk?"

"Trunk or chest. There was one where I was hiding. I didn't open it, but the coins were lying on the ground by it and there was nothing else there. Surely the coins came from inside it." She tented her fingers, her speech slower, more thoughtful. "Which brings us back to my original question—why was that man in the compound? Maybe he knew about the coins, heard your uncle was trying to sell them or something."

"It's possible." Daniel scratched his head. "Something else has been bugging me. Why did Varga go up there?"

"I only heard them mention el Padre."

"So was el Zopilote supposed to be there?" He rubbed a hand against his jaw. "But if he was the buyer, why didn't he take it? Why would someone tell you it would be on this ship?"

"I don't know." She frowned.

"Could your information about this cruise be wrong?"

"Not likely."

She sounded so definite he didn't pursue that angle.

"I wonder if the statue is being used as a cover to transport something else. Uncle Bert told me the crime syndicates down here have grown much more powerful. If Varga is transporting drugs—" Daniel paused, uncertain as to where he was going with this.

"Why would he pick a stolen statue to do it." Sam lay back on the lounger, closed her eyes and basked in the sun's warmth. "That sounds crazy."

"I guess." Though there were tons of people aboard, the sun and the ocean's slapping waves offered solace and time to think. Content to share the atmosphere, Daniel sat beside her as his heart mourned the loss of the only person who'd ever said they loved him. Life would be so empty without Uncle Bert.

"I needed him here, God, with me," he prayed silently. "I need his counsel, his love and support, his constant prayers. Why did You let him die?"

Remember one thing, Daniel. It doesn't matter whether I'm physically present. What matters is that I hold you in my heart. Because of our faith in God, we will never be separated. Bert's words, scrawled across the bottom of his letter now returned with haunting clarity, as if he'd somehow known.

"Daniel?"

He blinked, refocused on Sam. She wore a look on her face that told him she'd called his name more than once. "Yes?"

"A man's been watching us."

"Who?" He picked up his drink, sipped it and then pretended to reposition his chair.

"Up on top. Where the walking track is. He's been staring this way for a while." She pulled out a compact and pretended to check her makeup. "Maybe I've got a hole in the back of my head."

"If you do it's well hidden. You look beautiful, Samantha. You always did, but now…" He let that go and started over. "That makeup is the best disguise I've ever seen, makes your eyes look very mysterious."

"Thanks, *honey,*" she murmured as another couple sat down near them.

He brushed a finger down her cheek then casually glanced in the direction she'd indicated. There was a man standing there, but his binoculars were trained on something else now. "White shirt, blue pants?" he asked.

"That's the one."

"Then let's give him a show." Daniel leaned forward, allowed one jet black curl to twist itself around his finger. "Go along with me," he begged softly before brushing his lips against her cheek. "Our charade begins. I wish I had a camera."

"I've got one in my suitcase, but for now I'll use my phone, send the picture to Finders. Maybe we can get an ID."

"Good idea."

Her performance was flawless. She took out her phone, made him pose just so, then adjusted her view. "All finished."

People watched, smiled, then turned away, obviously accepting them as one of the group.

"Your photography's off. I don't even show up in that picture," he teased, peering over her shoulder at the screen.

"Because I already know who you are, Daniel."

But you don't, he wanted to say. *You don't know me at all.* He didn't say it. What was the point? She'd made it clear that day in his office that she wasn't interested. He rose.

"Are you going somewhere?"

"To the cabin. I want to check my laptop. I might be away but Finders, Inc. goes on." He also wanted to e-mail the mission department, see if he could get any new information about Bert.

"I'll go with you." She held out a hand, allowing him to pull her up. "I'm sure there'll be plenty of time to sunbathe on this cruise." She looped her arm through his, offered him a dazzling smile that almost convinced him they were a loving couple. "I need to unpack anyway. Those dresses will be crushed if they stay in that suitcase much longer."

Daniel walked beside her up the stairs to their suite, glad of the exercise that kept his mind from dwelling on the pretense he'd suggested. They received several smiling nods from other couples who seemed to think they were the picture of bliss. Good thing they didn't know the truth.

The game lasted until the suite door closed behind them. Sam pointed to one door. "I'll take this room, okay?"

"Sure. Doesn't make a difference to me." He pointed to her suitcase. "Can I have that camera?"

"What for?"

"I'm going to scout around the ship, see what I can find. I'd like to take pictures of some of the other passengers and see if Finders has anything juicy on any of them."

"Oh." She dug through her things and dragged out a small digital camera she'd purchased in Lima. "Here."

"Thanks." It was awkward, pretending to be so close, then trying to bridge the chasm when they were alone. "I'll see you in about a half hour. That should give us enough time to dress for dinner."

"It's not fancy tonight. First nights never are." She flushed at his look. "I read it in the brochure."

"I see." His fingers closed around the doorknob. He needed to get out, to find breathing space and concentrate on something other than Samantha.

"Daniel?"

"Yes?"

"There's something you should know."

"Okay." He didn't like the way she said it, as if she didn't want to tell him some secret but felt compelled.

"A friend of mine, Ric Preston, knows why I'm in South America."

He froze. Turning to face her, he asked, "How does he know that?"

"Ric used to work for the CIA. We've met several

times. Actually he helped me out after the jungle incident, before you got here. He's in Lima on a case of his own. He runs his own business—much like ours only smaller." She looked at him and swallowed.

"I see."

"Anyway, we were talking about our work and Ric said he'd already heard rumors about an Inca statue, so I wasn't giving anything away. When I mentioned I was tracking it, he said he'd make some inquiries, see if anyone knew who was buying."

"You may have blown your investigation." Anger surged through him like a tidal wave. Anger, and maybe a touch of jealousy for the faceless Ric. "How well do you know this guy?"

"Well enough. Ric isn't a bad guy." Her chin jutted out. "Just because he doesn't work for Finders, Inc. doesn't make him the enemy."

"It doesn't make him an ally, either. We don't know what's going on. Until we do, it would be preferable to keep any further info we get between the two of us. Agreed?"

She nodded, her eyes glittering with temper.

Daniel dragged open the door before he said something more damaging. "Maybe he is a good guy, but you can't afford to let your personal feelings influence you."

"At least I have some. I'm not an icicle like you." She was really angry. "The thing about Ric is that he's a man who appreciates that I have a fully functioning brain. He doesn't constantly question my actions, criticize me for not always doing things his way."

"I wasn't doing that, Samantha." Daniel closed the door on whatever else she had to say. He didn't want to hear any more about Sam's perfect friend, or his own mistakes.

A brochure from the steward explained the layout of the ship. Daniel located the spot where Sam had seen the man earlier. He was gone now, but the position did offer a great view of the ship's stern. The question was why he'd chosen it.

Daniel paced the upper decks, mentally putting pieces of the case together and pulling them apart when they didn't fit. But no matter how many details he fed his brain, it returned to the memory of Sam's face when she'd talked about Ric Preston. She had blushed when she said his name. Her eyes had softened and her mouth had turned up in a tiny smile she'd never worn for him.

A stab of pain taunted him for his own foolishness. He'd reamed her out for allowing personal feelings, yet he was doing the same. Concentrate on the job.

He pulled out his cell phone, text-messaged a memo to Shelby at Finders. Ric Preston—ex-CIA. Need info fast. It made good business sense to find out everything he could about the guy before they proceeded any further. Life had taught Daniel to trust only after verifying. Apparently Sam had picked up on that, because she didn't trust him at all.

Samantha pretended to admire the ocean view from her balcony, but in fact she never saw a thing. Her mind was too busy replaying Daniel's dismayed expression when she'd told him about Ric. She couldn't afford to be stubborn about accepting help. It wasn't as if she was making much progress. Her phone rang.

"Hey, it's me."

"Ric!" The sound of his voice was a welcome pleasure. Tension drained away as she pictured that good-looking face, imagining the quirk of his mouth tipped up in a lazy smile. "Where are you?"

"Top secret, Sammy." He chuckled. "I got some info for you. My sources tell me there's to be an auction on your cruise ship. One of the items to be sold will be a certain statue."

"I read that it's a gold auction." She waited but he said nothing. "The statue isn't gold, Ric."

"Don't know about that." It sounded like he was among a lot of people. "Maybe the gold's underneath."

"Could be. I'll take a look if I get a chance. Thanks."

"Welcome. Take care, Sam. By the way who's with you?"

"Top secret," she shot back. "If I told you, I'd have to hurt you."

Ric laughed, clicked off.

Samantha was halfway to her own room when a noise at the door startled her. The doorknob wiggled a couple of times. Daniel.

"Just a minute," she called. "I've got the lock on." She slid the chain off, pulled open the door. "Sorry, I—"

All she could see was white as a cloth moved over her mouth. She struggled to free herself, but the fingers on her arm tightened as the room melted and began to meld into a patch of beige. Sam grasped the arm, tried to force it away. Her fingers closed on something and she held on for dear life.

"We want the merchandise."

She didn't recognize the voice, but she knew she was in trouble. With what little strength she had left, Sam thrust out her arm, stretched as far as possible until her fingertips hovered over her phone. She'd thought the panic button mentioned during the fire drill a needless frill, but if she hit it surely someone would come. Summoning every ounce of strength, she stretched the last inch and pressed with the tip of her finger.

"You shouldn't have done that," the voice said as a screeching alarm filled the room. "We'll only come back. We want what you took."

Sam could offer no response, nor could she stop herself from crumpling to the floor. The room went black.

FIVE

"Are you all right, Samantha?"

Something must be really wrong for Daniel to use her full name. Sam blinked. She was on her bed. Daniel sat beside her, his hand warm where it brushed against her brow.

Her mouth felt dry as cotton wool and she licked her lips. "What happened?"

"That's what we'd like to know. The steward found you lying on the floor, passed out. The door was open and the alarm going."

Like the dregs of a nightmare it came back, the fingers pinching her shoulder, the cloth smothering her.

"Someone broke in," she told him, suddenly aware that there was more than one interested pair of eyes in the room, watching her. "He grabbed me. I managed to hit the panic alarm then blacked out. I'm sorry, I didn't get a look at him."

Daniel glanced at the purser, who immediately turned to someone Samantha assumed was security. They murmured together.

"Since she doesn't need a doctor, we'll leave, check around, and see if anyone noticed anything." They gave her one last cursory look then hurried away. The steward held out a tumbler, which Daniel accepted and lifted toward her lips.

"It's lemonade, Sam. Would you like a drink?"

"Yes, please." She sat up, leaned toward the glass and sipped, allowing the icy lemon flavor to slide down her throat. "Thank you. I can get up now. I'm fine."

Daniel nodded at the steward and the man quietly left the room, pulling the door closed behind him. Daniel held out a hand, his eyes intent as he watched her stand. "Okay?"

"I'm fine." She grasped the back of a chair to steady herself. "They put a cloth over my mouth. Some kind of drug, I'm guessing. I feel muzzy, as if I'm coming out of some anesthetic."

His lips tightened. "This is getting weirder by the moment."

"He said they wanted the merchandise," she murmured, remembering the husky demand.

"Do you mean those two coins?" Daniel's eyes burned a deep burnished gold. "Someone followed you on board for that?"

"No one followed, I checked. The guy with the binoculars was a new face." She began to shake her head, stopped. "If he wanted my coin he could have taken it." She pointed to the nightstand where the gold disk lay.

"He was in here?"

"No," she admitted wearily. "I don't think so." Sam searched for some other explanation. "Merchandise. It could mean anything."

"You're sure you didn't pick something up. Think, Sam."

"I picked up three coins. One I gave to the bus driver.

One I sent to you. It's with the other one—there." She frowned. "The man who attacked me—he had the nicest hands. Smooth, clean manicured nails."

"Okay." Daniel gave her a strange look.

"Don't ask me why I remember that but I do."

He shrugged. "Not much to go on. Half the men on this ship probably have regular manicures. You should see some of the pinkie rings."

"I'll pass, thanks." She rubbed her temple where a faint pounding had begun. "I'm hungry."

"Why don't you change, then we'll go up on deck, get something to eat and see if we can spot anything unusual."

She nodded. "Okay."

"What's in your hand?"

"Huh?" Samantha glanced down, saw that her fingers were clenched. She let them unfold slowly, surprised to see a scrap of white fabric in her palm. Her brain flashed back to that arm reaching out, covering her mouth. She'd grabbed it and hung on as tightly as she could.

Daniel picked it off her palm, turned it over. "Looks like we're dealing with someone on staff." He pointed to the metal button still attached. "That's off a uniform. The button carries the crest of the cruise line."

A shiver of unease skated over Sam's nerves. She met Daniel's knowing stare and licked her dry lips.

"There's no way to tell who it was," she whispered. "He could show up anytime he wants. No one would suspect if one of the staff was in the room."

"Which is the reason we'll stick together like glue. When we're outside of here, we're inseparable." He gripped her hand, squeezed. "Got it?"

She nodded, decided not to comment on his tone. In

her heart she knew he was right. But the prospect of him hovering over her while she tried to do her job wasn't easy to swallow. Independence had always been her strength. Until now she'd never needed anyone to watch her back.

Daniel slipped the evidence into his pocket. "It's obvious your disguise didn't matter. Someone already knew you were on board, even knew which room you were in."

"Not hard if you're on staff, I guess." Nothing seemed real. Was that an effect of the drug?

"There's something that puzzles me about this whole thing." Daniel pulled open the patio door to let in the sea air. "You left the jungle. You got on a bus. You didn't notice anyone following?"

She shook her head.

"And you weren't carrying anything. So why do they think you've got this merchandise? Where would you put it? It would make more sense if you'd tried to sell something, get some money from the first place you could hock them. But why trail you here?"

"I don't know." That voice—she let it play through her brain over and over. *We want our merchandise.* Why not say coins? "Could you sell the coins on the open market, Daniel? There must be laws about recovered bounty."

"There are. If the coins were inside that trunk you saw, I'm guessing Bert had them stashed for a good reason. I think I'll ask Shelby to send out some feelers, see if anybody's talking about them." He shook his head, sighed. "The puzzle has yet another knot." He kept looking at her.

"More than you know," she admitted. "Ric called. He says a source told him there's going to be an auction on board—of a certain statue."

"Good old Ric. Always in the know. Except that we already guessed that." He kept staring at her with the steady, unnerving scrutiny that seemed to penetrate soul deep. "Who's his source?"

"No idea. But he wouldn't have bothered to call me if it wasn't credible." Sam wished she hadn't told him. She was sick of being second-guessed.

"So if the statue's intact, what merchandise are your pals after?" He sat down, dropped his head back and closed his eyes. "Let's look at this from another angle. Maybe some of the natives took coins from Bert's hideout."

"I don't think they knew they were there. Nonee didn't seem to notice the ones on the floor. She was too afraid. They all were. No one even looked at me when I left. Who could blame them? Their lives were in ruins. Some of their men were hurt, some huts burned." The utter devastation was crystal clear in her mind.

"Did my uncle say anything before—before he died?"

"Just that he didn't have what el Zopilote wanted." Certainty filled her. "Daniel, if those people loved him as much as you say, they would have gotten the coins to save his life. If they knew about them. Something's off."

"Probably my stomach," he joked as the rumble was too loud to ignore. "I'm starved. Can we get something to eat now?"

"Sure." Sam grabbed her sweater, tucked the camera in her bag and followed him out the door. "Shall we try the dining room?"

"Might as well get a look at who we're traveling with." He followed her up the stairs then stood behind her in the doorway of the dining room while they waited to be seated. "At least we got a fairly central table," he murmured after the maître d' had seated them. "And it's for two. That seems to be a rarity. Recognize anyone?"

Sam glanced around. "No. I don't see Obrigado, but he wouldn't necessarily come here for the first meal of the cruise. He has a reputation as a high flyer." She picked up the menu card. "I hope there aren't a lot of seafood choices, though considering our location I guess that's rather silly."

"Ah, the allergies. I remember. You could copy me—I'm having the steak. Maybe that will give me some energy. I feel like I'm sleepwalking."

"Jet lag. I guess you're not used to this life anymore."

"Meaning I'm soft, Samantha?" His eyes dared her to agree.

"I didn't say that." She waited until they'd placed their orders then grinned at him. "Don't you ever wish you were back in the field?"

"Quite often actually." Daniel studied his salad for several moments before raising his head. "Sometimes I've dreamed of just disappearing, never listening to that phone ring again. I miss the anonymity. But Shelby needed me at Finders, Inc. and I was happy to help."

"I'm sure she was very grateful. But Shelby's got Tim now." How did Daniel feel about their boss's new marriage? He'd always seemed protective of Shelby, almost fatherly. Sam had never understood the bond between them.

"I'm delighted she and Aimee have Tim. She's asked me to stay in my position a little longer, so I will. I want her to have all the time she needs." He poked at the iceberg lettuce, his face contemplative. "She and Grant were my best friends. Grant would have wanted me to make sure they were settled, adjusting. I'll help Shelby any way I can. For now, that's running the company. And if that includes cruising the Galapagos Islands with you then I'm happy to suffer for the company." He offered her a funny little grin.

"I probably shouldn't have told you to come," she admitted. "It's just that I—well, truthfully, I was sure you could shed some light on that coin. I thought I was missing something. Following that statue all over the place was bad enough, but in the jungle—"

"You stumbled into something else?" He tilted one eyebrow.

"Or I was drawn in. This case isn't like my others. I can't get a feel for it. I'm always off-kilter somehow." She hated saying it, because she was certain he'd believe he'd been right to deny her that promotion. But she needed his perspective.

"That's unusual for you. Your instincts are usually dead-on."

"Thanks." She sipped her water. "Maybe it's Varga. He has been acting weird from the beginning."

"Weird how?" He waited till the salad bowl was removed.

"Furtive," she mused. "Other times he overacted, made stupid mistakes like a rookie would do. If he wanted me to have the statue he could have dropped it anywhere. Instead he trailed all over the place with it." She picked up her fork and plunged it into the baked potato in frustration. "I don't get why."

"Sounds to me like he wanted you to stick to him."

"Because?" She tasted the dressing.

"To keep you from following someone else?"

"I don't know." Sam blinked. "He made these night assignations sometimes. Somebody would appear, they'd talk. I never got close enough to hear what about, but Varga wasn't a happy camper even though he took the money he was offered. I figured he'd made a deal, but then he'd always take the statue back from the other guy and off we'd go again." She shook her head. "It sounds crazy but that's what happened." She savored the veal cutlet, only then realizing how hungry she was.

"Once I followed a peddler all through Turkey. Most frustrating assignment I ever had. The guy had a monkey with a little pouch. He'd stop and talk to people, they'd pet the monkey, and then he'd move on. It was ages before I figured out he was selling drugs." Daniel crunched on an ice cube, his attention on something in the past. "You want the truth? Sounds to me like the statue is Varga's monkey."

Sam leaned forward, her curiosity aroused. "Why do you say that?"

"The statue's too visible." He snapped his fingers. "Maybe there's something inside it."

"Interesting. Ric suggested maybe I'd find gold underneath the pottery."

"Huh." He was silent for a few moments then looked at her sideways. "Could there be another player in this game, Sam?"

"Besides the men at your uncle's compound, el Zopilote and Varga, you mean?" she asked, surprised by his question. "Like who?"

"Maybe your Ric."

"He's not *my* Ric, Daniel." A rush of anger swamped her and she set down her fork with a clang. "I've already told you—Ric is a friend. He isn't interested in the statue or what we're doing."

"Keep up the facade, honey," he warned softly.

"You said it hadn't done any good." Sam took another drink of her water.

"Tell me, how do you know Ric isn't interested in the statue?" Daniel's face remained expressionless, but he had that knowing look in his eye. "Because he told you?"

"Among other reasons."

"I had him checked out, Samantha." His jaw flexed and hardened. "The CIA doesn't claim Ric." His eyes never left her face.

"I told you—he *used* to work for them. Besides, if he was working covert in those days, they wouldn't go around telling people, now would they?" She met his stare, forcing her voice to modulate while she quashed down the bubble of fury inside. "Why did you ask Finders to investigate my friend, Daniel? Do you think I'm incapable of judging who is and is not trustworthy?"

"I never thought that at all. I simply prefer to check out everyone who's connected to a case." He laid down his fork and knife. Leaning back in his chair, he said, "Standard operating procedure."

"Bully for you." She fumed inwardly at his smug tone. "I do not investigate my friends," she hissed after the server had removed their plates. "The difference between us is that I don't expect my friends to betray me."

"I didn't realize he was that good a friend. If I've offended you, I'm sorry."

Despite his meek words, Daniel McCullough didn't look sorry. He looked smug. Superior and self-satisfied.

"I don't want—"

"Let's put off this discussion till later, shall we, dear?" He beamed when the waiter offered a delicate chocolate cheesecake. "We'll certainly have a piece of that."

It tasted like sandpaper to Sam. She swallowed a few

bites, sipped the coffee he ordered and wished profoundly that she'd never asked for his help. If she knew Daniel, and she did, once he was through "investigating," Ric wouldn't look at her sideways.

"Shall we go for a stroll?"

Sam rose without saying a word, and she let him lead her from the room. Still silent, they walked to the prow and the uppermost deck of the ship where the public was allowed. Groups of people were scattered here and there.

"You still haven't seen Obrigado?"

She shook her head. "He may be on the late seating for dinner." She leaned against the rail and stared into the ocean below.

"Beautiful, isn't it?" His tone had changed, the harshness evaporated. "Water and I have always had a connection. Uncle Bert used to call the South Pacific at night black velvet. Sometimes we'd moor in the shallows and swim after dinner. He said it felt like slipping on velvet gloves. I loved those evenings together with him. I never thought a day would come when—"

Daniel didn't finish. His face was in shadow, hiding his expression, but Sam knew he was feeling his loss of the man he'd never see again.

"He sounded very compassionate and kind when I was hurt." How did one help someone as strong as Daniel? "I've never felt someone radiate love but he did."

"He was like that. Gentle, warm. As a kid I always knew I could ask him anything and he'd help me. He was like a father."

"Better than your own father?"

"Oh yeah." He laughed a harsh, biting sound that sounded angry in the softness of the night. "On his best days my father was never gentle or warm. He was about as hard-nosed as they come, and determined that his son would be the same. I'm afraid I was a grave disappointment to him. Not only did I not possess the killer instinct he did for the stock market, I hated everything about his world. And for that, I think he hated me."

"Daniel, I'm sure—"

He placed his fingers over her mouth, stopping the automatic response. Sam held her breath, glimpsing an ache that had never been healed and stymied by the knowledge. Daniel—vulnerable?

"You never met him so you couldn't know how he was," he said as his hand fell away. "Most people can't imagine that someone who was as famous for his friendliness as my father was could be cold. They never imagined it was all an act. But then they never saw the side of him that I did. Maybe that's where I got my ability at disguise."

"I'm sorry." She didn't know how to comfort him, but realized suddenly that she wanted to.

"Yeah. So am I." He straightened, twisting his head so she couldn't see his face. "Anyway, that's the past and hardly worth raking over again. The question is what do we do now? What is our goal for being here? Maybe we should reconsider what we've learned."

"Excuse me? Mr. McCullough?"

They hadn't even noticed the attendant come up behind them. Daniel raised one eyebrow. "Yes?"

"Come with me, please. The purser would like to speak to you."

"Can't it wait?" He winked at the other man. "You've provided this moonlight, a little breeze off the ocean, some music. I'm with this gorgeous lady. An opportunity like this doesn't come along every day."

The man never cracked a smile. "It won't take long, I assure you. Just a few minutes."

"What's this about?" Daniel turned the strength of his amber glare on the fellow and the other man shifted his stance.

"I'm just the steward, sir. I don't know anything except I'm to ask you to come immediately to his office."

"Tell him I'll come by later."

"I'm afraid I can't do that, sir. He was most insistent that he speak to you now."

"This better be important." Daniel bent to whisper in Sam's ear. "Maybe it's about your attack. You might as well come along. There's no point in waiting out here alone." He faced the steward. "She's coming, too."

"Whatever you say, sir."

Sam didn't get a chance to protest before Daniel's hand under her elbow urged her forward.

"If you'll both follow me this way, please." The steward held the chain for them to pass, and then secured it. "We'll use the staff stairway to reach his office. With the evening show about to begin the hallways are crowded. This will be much quicker."

He preceded them down the stairs and into a small passageway with several different doors. The narrowness of such an enclosed space irritated her but Samantha suppressed her discomfort. No way was Daniel going to see another flaw.

"I'll just open this and we'll go on through," the man said, standing before a door that read Staff. Sam noticed the tattered corner of his sleeve where a button was missing. Moving imperceptibly, she gained Daniel's attention. He nodded.

"You know, I've got a headache and this isn't helping.

I think we'll go back to our cabin. The purser can speak to us there."

Sam felt the hand on her back an instant after she saw Daniel stumble forward. She fell against him as the door closed behind them. Reflexes sent her springing to grab the door handle. It didn't budge.

"This cruise is really beginning to bug me," Daniel complained, rubbing his neck.

"Are you hurt?"

"He grabbed my chain, but it held. The coin's still here." He showed her, then eased past. "Let me look." But though he rattled the doorknob hard, it wouldn't open.

"He locked it." She'd noticed that a second after the door closed. Sam fought to maintain her calm. "Daniel?" Smoke filtered through a small grate on the side wall.

"Now I understand why he wanted to rush us in here. It's a trap." Daniel seemed unconcerned by the smoke; his attention remained on the door. "This lock has to be opened with a key. Strange they don't have an escape mechanism in case someone gets caught inside. Notice anything?"

She tried to focus. "The lock looks shiny, new."

"Uh-huh. I'd say someone planned this in advance."

"For one coin?"

"Maybe to get me out of the way with a bogus trip to the purser's office while they drag you in here?"

Sam hadn't even considered that. She clutched her fingers into her thighs as just above her head tiny white tendrils now curled across the ceiling like snakes set free. The walls seemed to be moving in.

"Daniel?"

"Yes?"

"I'll gratefully accept any and all suggestions for our next step."

He was silent a moment, examining the lock.

"You really want to hear my advice?"

She nodded.

"Pray."

SIX

If his math was accurate, Daniel figured they had about five minutes before the smoke overtook them.

He found his wallet, slid out a small pick and went to work on the door lock, delighted that for once Samantha didn't suggest she take over. In fact, she was strangely silent.

The dim wall light cast little illumination, so he had to work by feel.

"What are you doing?" She sounded breathy, nervous.

"Trying to unlock the door. Unfortunately my lock-picking skills are rusty. I don't use them much in the office." He glanced over his shoulder. Her face looked too white, and he noticed how the smoke created a halo around her head. At this rate it wouldn't be long before his view of the lock was obliterated.

Daniel began silently praying as he applied pressure to the tumblers. After several tries the mechanism finally popped. He shouldered open the door, pulled her into the hall and up the stairs. In the clear air Samantha began to draw in huge gasps of air. She put a hand to her head as if it were aching.

"Are you all right?"

"Yes." Her eyes were round and scared and he wanted nothing more than to hold her and soothe her worries. But Sam wouldn't want that. He had a hunch she didn't want him to know she was scared, either.

"Can our next cruise have rock-wall climbing?" he teased. "It would certainly be more restful."

She took it the wrong way. Her eyes grew stormy, her chin thrust out.

"This was not my fault, Daniel. But whatever else you want to bawl me out for will have to wait until tomorrow. I'm going to bed. Good night." She turned and walked away, her shoulders straight, rigid. But when she reached up to brush a strand of hair off her face, her hand was trembling.

Okay, so he'd blown it. Again. She was upset. It was little wonder she'd snapped at him. This case was getting stranger with every turn. Daniel trailed behind her, content to remain silent while he figured out how to get his foot out of his mouth.

The second seating for dinner was now in progress so the stairwells were almost deserted. It wasn't hard to follow Sam. They could have walked two abreast, but Daniel kept his distance, allowing her time and space to collect herself. When she rounded the last corner before their room, he held back, wondering if it wouldn't be a good idea to talk to the captain privately once she was locked in her room.

A moment later he heard her exclaim. "Oh! Excuse—you!"

Daniel straightened from his lounging position, every sense at the ready.

"What are you doing here?" she demanded.

"You know why I'm here."

The voice had no noticeable accent. Daniel wanted to get a look but was afraid the man would see him. Until something happened, he'd stay out of sight and learn what he could.

"If I knew why, Varga, I wouldn't ask. Why are you dressed like one of the staff?"

She had to know Daniel was there, so she must be making sure he understood the situation. He stayed where he was.

"I am here to do a job." The ingratiating tone thinned. "You have something. My boss wants it."

"You're the one who has something that doesn't belong to you. I want that statue and I'm not going to stop trailing you until I get it."

"This isn't about what you want," he said, so softly Daniel almost didn't hear. "It's about what you took."

"You just don't get it. I didn't take anything! I barely escaped with my life." Sam's scathing tone would have ripped flesh off lesser men. Then her voice dropped. "Do you seriously think I hauled something out of the jungle on my back as I was running from you murderers?"

Daniel risked a look around the corner. Varga's back was to him now. Sam saw him but gave nothing away facially. One hand, the one clutching her bag, moved. Two fingers came up in a "stay" motion.

"You've been lugging around a stolen statue. You ruined that village and almost everything in it and you stood by while someone else took a man's life. Don't talk to me about taking something."

"It's better to forget that day," he warned. "But better yet to remember the punishment. Return what you took or hand over the coins as payment." His lips pinched tighter. "Stop playing games, Ms. Henderson."

"You're one to talk about games, trailing all over the continent with a silly statue that you probably switched for a fake long before you left Rio."

His lips rolled back in a shark smile. "It took you long enough to catch on."

Daniel caught a glimpse of a knife blade flashing. He took a step forward, prepared to intervene if necessary, but Sam held her ground.

"El Señor wants what is his. He is not a patient man."

"Whatever he wants, I haven't got. I have one gold coin. Will that satisfy you? No?" She shook her head, her smile as sarcastic as her voice. "Too bad. That's all I have. Now let's talk about what I'm after, which is that stolen statue."

"Perhaps the statue could be yours," he insinuated, then paused as another couple entered the hallway. He waited until they were safely inside their stateroom before leaning forward so his face was inches from hers.

Daniel's protective instincts inched higher, but he stayed where he was, waiting for her signal.

"Get the coins and perhaps el Señor will trade."

So Varga really didn't know where the coins were. Daniel stored that information away for later.

"Why would you think I'd have access to them?"

He smiled. "You are a very beautiful woman, Ms. Henderson, but even such a beautiful lady does not always have someone following her every move unless there is a reason."

Someone following her—him? Daniel blinked.

"You don't understand. Daniel's here to help me find the statue. For our customer."

Varga simply smiled.

"Believe what you want, but I repeat—I don't have

your coins. I don't know where they are. All I'm here for is to recover the statue that was stolen from my client."

A burst of loud laughter echoed down the hall. Someone was coming. Varga stepped back.

"I advise you to consider wisely, Ms. Henderson. And consider one thing more. El Señor does not like the word 'no.'" He stared at her for one long moment. "But I think you know this already." He half bowed and left.

"Well, that was…curious." Daniel walked toward her.

Sam blinked as if she'd been deep in thought. "Yeah."

"Did you notice his left cuff?" He waited for her negative response as he opened the door to their room. "Button's missing. My guess is he's the one who drugged you."

"Because he wants the coins, in lieu of some other 'merchandise' they didn't get when they were in your uncle's camp." She shook her head. "Varga didn't drug me. I'd have recognized his voice. But he knew I was in the jungle and he knew I saw Bert being killed. And he works for el Señor. So is that the name of the man in the camp, and if it is, who is el Zopilote?" She walked past him into their suite. "Which brings me to my next question."

"Let's see if we're thinking along the same lines." Daniel closed the door, locked it, pulled off his tie and sank onto one of the upholstered chairs. "What was it they were originally looking for, and what does it have to do with my uncle?"

"Good questions."

"Got any answers?"

"No." Samantha slid open the balcony door to let in some fresh air. She paused there, staring at him. "But I have more questions. Did you hear him talk about someone following me?"

"He meant me." Daniel wished desperately that this conversation would take a different turn.

"That's what I thought, at first." Sam nodded. "But he said following me, not with me." Her gaze narrowed. "Did you have someone traipsing around after me, boss?"

Her eyes glittered like polished bits of emerald shard signaling her anger. But then he'd gone into this expecting Sam to learn more than he wanted.

"I put someone on you when you first arrived, yes. But after your initial check-in, he stopped reporting. That must be at least three weeks ago."

"A babysitter, Daniel?" Her fingernails bit into the fabric back of the chair she stood behind. "Thanks for the confidence."

"It's routine, Sam. I do it for every new assignment."

"Save it." The bitterness in her face matched her voice. "I've been on a number of missions. I've never seen anyone before."

"You weren't supposed to," he said quietly, meeting her glare. The truth was it had always been a matter of routine in the past: note the agent's arrival and wait for reports. With Sam he'd been on tenterhooks.

"Varga's implication that someone was following me could mean this body you sicced on me."

"Hardly sicced, and since you didn't notice I doubt he did. Anyway, he said *following,* as if it was happening present tense, not three weeks ago."

Daniel saw her forehead pleat and knew she was working through something. He decided to hear her out before saying any more. After all, technically, this was her operation. He bent over, untied his shoes and slipped them off. "Go on."

"He wants the coins. Since he hasn't got them, they

must still be in the jungle. I'm going to take him up on his trade."

"You can't!"

"Can't I?" Her flashing glare dared him to argue. "I have no more clues about the statue. If it doesn't show up on this ship, I've hit a dead end. Varga's willingness to trade makes me wonder if the statue is worth a penny."

"How do you propose to organize this trade?"

"I don't know yet. Varga talked about his boss. Maybe he's on the cruise." She drew a thin golden chain from her bag. The coin was attached. "If I flash this around and there's someone aboard who's interested, we should notice."

She would be making herself the trap and Daniel didn't like it one bit. "Don't mistake genuine interest for greed, Sam."

"I think I can discern the difference." She turned toward her room, opened the door. "Good ni—oh, no!"

"What's wrong?" Daniel surged to his feet and hurried over. Garments were strewn everywhere. "Forget to tidy up?" he asked.

"No. I hung up all those beautiful clothes." She walked to the closet then checked inside. "Someone's been in here."

He stood behind her, staring at the chaos. A black leather bag was almost shredded, as was her suitcase.

"I'm calling the purser." He strode toward the phone, grabbed it. Sam's hand clapped over his.

"Wait."

"For what?"

"I need to check a few things first." She took the phone from him, hung it up, then moved to the patio doors. "Was this locked? I didn't unlock it before I opened it, did I?"

"No—maybe." Frustration nipped at him. "I didn't pay any attention. Don't you remember?" He met her glare. If looks could incriminate...

"I don't think it was locked. Okay, the door next." She opened it, checked both ways down the hall, then squatted to stare at the latch. "I can't see any markings, but this isn't the most substantial door on the planet. A good shove or a lock pick would be equally effective."

"Or Varga's passkey, since apparently he's working on this ship. Now can I call the purser?"

She shrugged. "I guess. At the least the cruise line should cover the cost of the luggage."

"That's not what I'm worried about." Daniel picked up the phone, waited to be connected, then repeated their story. Ten minutes later the suite was brimming with staff who seemed truly shocked by the break-in.

"I assure you we have never had such a thing happen on our ship," the purser insisted. "It is most regrettable."

"It's not the only bad experience we've had aboard." Daniel related the incident regarding their imprisonment in the smoky room and received a promise that the offender would be found. An hour later Daniel and Sam were informed that the purser's inquiries had not found results.

"I didn't expect anything else. I've got some things to do, but you really should go to bed," he murmured when the silence between them had stretched too long.

"Yes." Her face reminded him of when they'd been locked in. "I hope you won't think I'm weak or inefficient, Daniel, but would you mind stuffing that chair under the doorknob before you retire? I'd prefer to keep our nocturnal visitors to a minimum."

"I'll look after it. Don't worry."

"I'm not worrying." She gave him an arch look chock-full of meaning. "I'm very well used to looking after myself. What I'm not used to is having someone check on my every move or send someone to follow me."

"I was doing my job, Sam. Just as you're doing yours."

Her bare feet curled into the carpet as she walked across the room. Her cap of glossy black curls shimmered in the overhead light, the tendrils caressing her cheeks as she stared at him.

Daniel tried to think of something to say, some innocuous remark that would keep her here a few minutes longer, something that would kill this great yawning chasm between them. He came up with nothing.

"Good night, Daniel." The door snapped closed behind her and he was left alone with his thoughts.

Too wide-awake to sleep, he secured the main entry as she'd asked, then escaped to the balcony, peering down each side to study the structure. It wasn't likely a thief would choose this route, which left him back at square one.

Though the night was dark, the ship's lights created enough illumination for him to glimpse other passengers enjoying the fresh breeze from their own private spaces along the side of the ship. The soft murmur of voices filtered over the water punctuated by happy laughter.

Daniel lowered himself into a deck chair, propped his feet on the railing and slid off his glasses as he replayed the events that had brought him here. After a moment he lifted one hand to touch the golden disk lying against his chest.

Small golden coins, forged and stamped years before, when no one had guessed that Samantha Henderson and Daniel McCullough would even exist. Yet what a lot of problems those coins had caused.

Especially for Uncle Bert.

That thought reminded him of the request he'd sent this morning that Shelby find out what she could about his uncle's remains and pending funeral arrangements by the mission. He checked his text messaging. Letter arrived from uncle. Shall I send it?

Bert had written him again? A faint breeze skittered over the back of his neck, raising the hairs there. When and why?

He'd held back his emotions too long. Now as Daniel closed his eyes and let the past play like a big-screen movie in his mind, he knew he'd been blessed. Bert wouldn't want him to be sad; he was with the God he'd served so faithfully. Bert didn't need Daniel. Did Sam?

His mind conjured the image of her lying unconscious on the floor and he knew the answer. In that moment, Daniel made up his mind. He messaged back: Hold letter till I return, then pocketed his phone. His fingers brushed the small Bible his uncle had given him for Christmas. He pulled it out, let it fall open.

> Therefore I say unto you, do not worry about your life, what you will eat or what you will drink, nor about your body, what you will put on. Is not life more than food and the body more than clothing… Consider the lilies of the field and how they grow; they neither toil nor spin; and yet I say to you that even Solomon in all his glory was not arrayed like one of these. Now if God so clothes the grass of the field which today is, and tomorrow is thrown into the oven, will He not much more clothe you, O you of little faith?

The message was clear—God was in control. Daniel only had to trust. Weariness, mingled with a sensation of emptiness, dragged at him. All his life he'd been able to act, to do something to make things better. Now suddenly he was helpless, forced to wait. It was a horrible feeling, one only alleviated by a vow that he would find out the truth behind his uncle's death before he left this continent. No matter what.

Daniel rose, locked the balcony doors and checked the main entrance again. After leaving a small lamp burning, he retired to his own room, stretched out on his bed and prayed for guidance to answer one question.

Who was after the coins?

"Bartolome Island is a tiny island of just 1.2 square kilometers. It is a combination of volcanic rock formations, the most famous being Pinnacle Rock."

The chatty tour guide led them up the wooden walkway onto steps that supposedly were an easy climb. The signs said their walk would reach 340 feet above sea level. Lava tubes and flows made up the landscape, but once they reached the summit the panoramic vista of Bartolome and the neighboring islands captivated the group.

"It's quite a view."

"Fantastic! See there. Penguins at the equator! I can hardly wait to do some snorkeling in those tidal pools." Samantha grabbed his hand and leaned closer to whisper, "I haven't seen a sign of Varga at all."

"Good." He met her dubious look with a grin. "He'd spoil the view." He held on to her hand when she would have pulled away, drew her up a final slope. "I can't figure out how Darwin could see all this and stick to his theories. It's obvious that only God could put this paradise together, that it didn't just happen to evolve."

"Mmm." She sat down on a rock, rested her elbows on her knees and her chin on that. "It looks a little like the surface of the moon up here with all this volcanic landscape. Except for that cactus."

"Cactus?" He glanced around.

"There, by those spatter cones. The guide said that particular type is only found on Galapagos."

"Oh." Daniel was more interested in watching Sam. She'd pressed the dancing curls off her face this morning allowing the sun to kiss her cheeks. The white shorts displayed her long slim legs perfectly while the candy-striped shirt concealed the swimsuit he knew she wore beneath.

"Are you ready to leave? I'd like to get in the water and see those parrot fish the guide talked about." She jumped up suddenly, her face a picture of horror.

"What?" Daniel looked down then burst out laughing. "It's not a crocodile, Sam. It's just a little lava lizard."

"Right. I'm going now," she grumbled, her cheeks red.

He forced himself not to laugh as she whirled around and headed for the path back down. Tough, determined to face Varga and his hoods—but scared by a little lizard. Oh, Sam.

A snorkeling area at the base of Pinnacle Rock hosted a female sea lion that swam circles around them, to Sam's giggles of delight. After they'd submerged, Daniel pointed out the glowing parrot fish that turned an orange eye on them. Green sea urchins, blue-eyed damsels, and sturgeon eating coral off the rocks—they coexisted happily.

When a white-tipped reef shark emerged from the

murky water and slid toward them, Sam grabbed Daniel's arm, her eyes wide with terror. He shook his head, wrapped his arms around her and held her still as the five-foot-long fish floated past. There were two more that followed and by the time Daniel had drawn her to the surface, Sam was shaking.

"Those were sharks!"

He nodded. "Yes. But unless you bother them, they aren't usually interested in you."

"I am not comforted by that, Daniel McCullough." Her eyes sparkled a warning, her voice sharp.

"Why don't you explore these tidal pools then? I want to go back in for a minute, see if I can see a hog streamer. There are supposed to be lots around here." He noted the subsiding shakes, checked her face. "Being under there didn't seem…claustrophobic?" he hinted.

"I'm fine. I simply don't like sharks." She turned her back, bent to explore a nearby pool. "Maybe I'll head back to the ship."

"Wait for me, Sam. I won't be longer than a few minutes." He swam out to deeper waters and began the search for his uncle's favorite fish. It seemed a fitting tribute.

But by the time he returned to the beach, Sam and her clothes were gone. He scanned the area, saw nothing and became annoyed. He'd only been gone—he checked his watched and blinked—half an hour? Daniel dragged on his clothes, returned the gear and headed for the ship. She was probably enjoying lunch.

But Samantha didn't show up for lunch and, as far as he could tell, she hadn't been back to their suite. Which meant she was either still on the island or somewhere on the ship. Since they were scheduled to leave in less than two hours he needed to find her.

Daniel went back to the gangplank, asked if she'd boarded. Security had no record of her return. So she was still on the island. He paused just long enough to notice that another ship had docked. If someone had managed to get her on that boat he might never find her—alive.

As Daniel studied a map, he made a decision. Pinnacle Rock—he'd have to climb it again to get a view of the entire island. He raced up the wooden walkway taking the steps two at a time, bypassing slower-moving folks who were there to appreciate the view. Sam was not among them, but then he hadn't expected her to be.

He paused every so often to catch his breath and survey the surrounding area. On the second stop he saw her, or thought he did. She was talking to someone whose back was to him, arguing as she waved her hand around.

Mindful of the volcanic tufa which the trail, wooden steps and boardwalk had been specially constructed to protect, Daniel kept to the path, working his way down as fast as he could. Every so often he paused for another glance. He saw the man grab her arm, trying to pull her forward. Sam resisted, tipped backward and fell. He could hear her cry from here. It impelled him toward her even faster.

By the time Daniel reached Samantha, the man was gone and she was wincing as she tried to brush away the baby cactus prickles from her clothes. He lent a hand.

"Are you all right?"

"No, I wouldn't say that, Daniel." Exasperated by his ineffectual efforts to remove the spines, she pushed his hand away. "I'm going back to the ship."

"I thought that's what you'd done in the first place," he complained, wondering if he'd looked as big a fool as he now felt. "We were supposed to stick together. You were supposed to wait. Who was that anyway? Your friend Ric?"

She stopped, turned and glared at him.

"Have you had too much sun? Ric isn't on the ship." She returned to her previous gait, pulling out the spines that still clung to her shorts.

"Who was it then?" He drew alongside her, noted how the curls had broken free of the band that had held them back and now tumbled all over her head. She was lucky she hadn't gotten them tangled in the cactus.

"I was on my way back to the ship when a man stopped me, said 'my boyfriend' had been injured by a shark and could I come quickly. I followed him until I realized he was not going to the beach area where we'd been. I ran in the other direction, slipped into a guided group of sightseers who were studying the lava formations. When they stopped to watch the penguins, I slipped away with another group and tried to go back to the beach, but the guy grabbed me from behind and I ended up in the cactus."

They boarded the ship and headed for their suite. Daniel stopped a passing valet and asked him to send a first-aid kit, then unlocked the door.

"What did this guy want?" he asked, when they were both inside and the door securely closed behind them.

Sam turned her back to him for a moment. When she turned around she was grinning.

"This." She opened her fingers to reveal the gold coin sitting in her palm. "He grabbed for my necklace and broke it but the coin slid inside my swimsuit."

A knock on the door stopped his protest. Daniel accepted the first-aid kit, turned down the suggestion to call for the ship's doctor and tipped the friendly steward. Then he faced Sam.

"Let's get the spines out," he told her, waiting while she pulled off her shorts and shirt to reveal her swimsuit beneath. "You're lucky. The fabric of that suit protected you from the worst." He began wielding the tweezers to remove the offending barbs, ignoring her yelps by clamping his lips together as he worked. One by one he tugged them out, then poured antiseptic over the wounds.

"You're enjoying this, aren't you?" she demanded several moments later, her face crumpling as one of the larger barbs tore a bit of flesh.

"Not in the least," he answered grimly, wondering how she'd feel if he leaned over and kissed the mark on her arm. "But leaving them in would be asking for trouble. Turn around."

She remained silent while he finished the job, even though removing the two on her calves and ankles must have stung like fury. When Daniel finally stood, Sam averted her head, hiding her expression.

"Is that all?" she whispered.

"Yes."

"Thank you. I'm going to have a shower." She was gone before he could protest. And she stayed gone for a very long time.

Daniel showered, changed into a suit and waited aeons. They'd agreed earlier to dress up for dinner tonight. So where was she?

"Sam?" He tapped on her door and waited. Surely she hadn't left by herself. He knocked, waited, then turned the knob and peeked inside.

She was asleep on the bed, wrapped in the thick white terry robe that matched the one hanging on his own bathroom door, dark hair curling damply against the pillow. One hand lay tucked under her cheek, the golden coin twinkling in the light from the bedside lamp.

"Samantha?" He sat down beside her, brushed his hand against her shoulder. "It's time for dinner."

"Hmm." She shifted, but her eyes did not open.

"Samantha." He couldn't resist the opportunity to touch her cheek, trail a finger across one eyelid, over the tip of her haughty nose, glide past her full lips to the stubborn tilt of her chin. "Come on, sleeping beauty. Dinner awaits."

"Daniel?"

Watching her waken was delightful. She blinked those incredibly spiky black lashes, leaned up on one elbow and frowned at him. "What are you doing?"

"Trying to rouse you so we can go have dinner." Her beauty stunned him.

"Oh." She smiled and licked her lips. "For a minute I thought you were a Galapagos penguin." She giggled when he tugged on a curl. "What time is it?"

"Um—"

She grabbed his wrist and pushed up his cuff to stare at his watch. "Good grief. Why didn't you wake me earlier? It'll take me ages."

"If it does we'll starve. We have only ten minutes until our seating."

"Out. Get out." She flew off the bed, disappeared into the bathroom, and then stuck her head out the door. "Which dress should I wear?"

"The green one." He didn't have to think twice. His mind would never forget Sam modeling that dress in the store. "Wear the green one."

"You're sure? It's so fancy." She wrinkled her nose. "But it will cover all my marks. Good thinking."

As if he'd been thinking about that!

"I'll be out in five."

"Sure you will. He chuckled as he pulled the door closed behind him.

But she was as good as her word, emerging from the bedroom in a cloud of scent that reminded him of Persia. Clothed in shadowy green, the dress resembled mist clouds against her pearly arms and shoulders, darkened to night shadows as it pooled on the floor around her feet.

"Well?" She turned around for his inspection. "Do I look okay?"

Okay? Try stunning.

"You look…very nice," he managed to say before he caught sight of the golden coin dangling from her wrist. "Are you sure that's a good idea?"

Samantha pulled open the door, beckoned to him, then, when he was beside her in the hall, threaded her arm through his.

"It's the perfect idea," she murmured in his ear as they walked down the stairs to the dining room, her excitement obvious. "Whoever is after this is going to know I still have it and they're going to come back for it, or at least to ask me about the rest."

"Hold it." He drew her to a halt in the doorway. "This isn't a game. He could really hurt you next time."

"Not while you're here to protect me." She grinned at him. "That isn't what you expected me to say, is it? Shock is written all over your face. It's kind of nice to know I'm not so predictable."

Samantha was in a strange mood. Daniel followed her to their table, well aware of the many heads that turned to look. He didn't blame them. Over the years he'd seen Samantha in many types of attire, but this one…

"Wake up, boss. You're staring at me." She reached across the table to pinch his arm.

"Everyone is staring at you." She was playing a part. He knew that. But even he could almost believe that soft glint of adoration in her eyes was for him alone. "Your dress reminds me of the forest at night—dark, mysterious and full of surprises."

Her eyebrows rose along with one corner of her lovely mouth, but she said nothing as she waited for her salad to be set before her. Once the server had left she leaned forward. A smile played with the corners of her lips.

"How poetic. Thank you. But you know me. Subtlety and mystery aren't my strong suits. I just want that statue. If I have to play their game to get it then I will. By the way, I specifically asked to be seated here."

"Why?"

"There's someone we need to meet."

"Excuse me?"

Daniel lifted his head to stare at the tall man who stood by their table. "Yes?"

"I am the maître d'. A gentleman at the table by the window has asked if you might join him and his wife for dinner this evening."

"I see." He glanced at Sam. She gave him a nearly imperceptible nod. So she knew this man. "What is the gentleman's name?"

"Señor Eduardo Sanchez," the man murmured. "He's the curator for the Inca museum in Lima."

Sam's nudge under the table told him she knew the guy.

"We'd be delighted to dine with Señor Sanchez tonight," he said, rising as he offered Sam his hand.

"This way please."

Judging by the amount of deference being shown, Daniel gauged Sanchez to be fairly important. Once introductions had been performed, Sanchez seated Sam next to him. Daniel sat beside Señora Sanchez, who apparently spoke little English. Indeed, the woman's focus seemed to be riveted on the South Pacific floating past their window.

Sam's gleaming smile told him she had something in mind for Señor Sanchez. Daniel would follow her lead.

"It's very kind of you to include us at your table, *señor.* Such kindness to strangers is part of South America's charm." Sam repeated almost the same thing in Spanish to the *señora,* who smiled.

"We welcome tourists," she agreed.

"More than welcome," Sam expounded. "I've run into difficulty several times during my stay here. People have been so generous in helping."

When the *señora* showed no further interest in the subject, Sam chatted about Pinnacle Rock until the main course was served. The *señora* remained silent. Not so her husband. His questions began innocently but soon expanded. What kind of business was Daniel in…what did Samantha do, etc. etc. Normal questions, until…

"What is that you wear upon your wrist?" Sanchez asked. After a moment he reached over and plucked the disk into his palm, thus holding Sam's wrist captive.

"A friend gave it to me," she told him. "Daniel has one, too. They were very special gifts."

Daniel opened his mouth to stop her, but the hard press of her pointed heel against his toe stopped him.

"It looks very old." The hint was obvious.

Samantha simply smiled, drew the coin from him and rubbed it against her cheek. "It may be," she murmured. "But we love it because of our friend, not because of its age."

"Ah, yes. Friends are rare gifts. One must treasure them."

Treasure. Daniel almost snorted, but Samantha's face remained impassive.

"True friends are very rare. So much in the world is built on greed and lust, money and evil. People do horrible things to get what someone else has. But justice and honesty are still much prized."

"You are after justice?" The words brimmed with foreboding.

"Me?" Samantha giggled. "Do you hear that, darling?" She grabbed Daniel's hand and squeezed. "As if I could bring about justice in the world! No, Señor Sanchez, seeing these beautiful islands and the wonders they hide—that will keep me happy. For now."

"You are a lucky man, then, Señor McCullough." Obviously relieved, Sanchez winked at Daniel. "Sometimes it is not easy to make a beautiful woman happy. Yes?"

"It's usually not that easy to keep Samantha happy. When she goes after something, she doesn't let anyone or anything get in the way."

"Is that so?" Sanchez frowned.

Daniel nodded, felt Sam's nudge against his ankle and knew she wanted him to stop pushing. Tough. If this was Varga's boss, he wanted to know and soon. Crème brûlées arrived. Daniel took Sam's with a big grin.

"What are you—"

"Darling, you can't eat that." If looks could kill... Daniel wrapped his fingers around hers and squeezed.

"You must keep that gorgeous figure for me." He grinned at Sanchez. "One must keep the man happy, too, no?"

The macho comment seemed to work, because Sanchez relaxed and grinned from ear to ear. If he kept this up, Daniel figured Sam would kick him and he'd deserve it. She made do with a glower but hid her temper, simply asking for a dish of fruit, which was served with a scoop of sorbet.

"I'm sure that's much healthier for you than this, honey," he murmured.

She raised one eyebrow.

"Anyway the cinnamon is too strong for my liking." He pushed away both dishes as understanding dawned in her expression.

"You shouldn't worry about me so much. It's only a mild allergy to cinnamon, after all," she told him quietly. "It's seafood that really does a number on my system."

"Just trying to help," he told her. "*Señor,* what brings you on this ship?"

Sanchez explained that he and his wife had been given the cruise as an anniversary gift. "Maria loves a chance to relax and enjoy the sun."

Could be true, but it was more likely that this sudden yearning for a sea trip somehow tied into the statue. They lingered over coffee. Sam conducted a scan of the diners while Daniel found a new topic.

"I wasn't sure if we should come on this cruise or not. Sam loves all things old. Sometimes my wallet can't keep up with her. I overheard someone talking about an auction that's to be held on board. Do you know which day?"

"Second to last, I believe." Sanchez pulled out a cigar, sniffed it. "You want to buy something special perhaps?"

"Oh, something very special. Samantha has been working so hard she deserves a treat. She loves anything Inca. Finished, darling?"

"Yes."

Daniel drew back her chair, admired the graceful way she rose, kept watching as her green dress became iridescent in the glow of chandeliers. "Perhaps we'll see you again, *señor, señora.* Thank you so much for sharing your table with us."

"We must talk again," Sanchez agreed, stumbling to his feet. "I, too, collect artifacts of the Inca period. Perhaps we can compare."

"Perhaps. Now if you'll excuse us, Daniel and I are due for a walk on deck."

"Ah, the young! Always thinking of the physical fitness." Sanchez waved a hand. "Go, enjoy the night." He said something to his wife who waved halfheartedly.

"Buenas noches."

"Good night."

Daniel led the way out, but once they were past the tables and into the hallway he lengthened his stride. Sam pulled on his arm, slowing him.

"These are four-inch heels, Daniel. Not exactly appropriate for running."

"Sorry." He punched the elevator button that would take them to the lookout deck. "I just wanted to get away. The smarm on that man was beginning to choke me." They stepped inside, glided up.

As she walked beside him on the smooth deck, her arm remained tucked in his. Daniel wouldn't change a thing as the night air danced past, sometimes pulling at their clothes, sometimes playing with their hair.

"A curator who happens to take this particular crui at the last minute, who despite his protestations is very interested in your coin. I'm not big on probability math, *darling,* but even I find that a stretch."

"He also 'happened' to know exactly when the auction would be held." Daniel paused beside the railing, stared at the full moon and ordered his brain to stop dwelling on the heady fragrance of her perfume and start putting together facts. "You're sure it wasn't Sanchez who stopped you on the beach?"

"I'm sure." Sam's fingers clutched his lapels. "Daniel, look! Porpoises. They're following us."

For a long time Daniel watched Sam watch the fish and counted himself lucky to be with her. Always before there'd been a barrier between them, one he'd tried to surmount a hundred times, without success. It was as if she'd resented him for something. But at the moment, there was no sign of that. Tonight they were just Sam and Daniel.

"Isn't it gorgeous?" She turned to face him, her eyes alive with excitement. "The water looks phosphorescent with the moon shining so brightly. It's like being in the middle of paradise and—" She paused, touched his cheek. "You look pensive."

"Not really." He turned his lips into her palm. "At this moment in time I'd say I'm utterly aware of just how precious life is."

"Oh." She glanced at her hand then continued to stare at him, her head tipping to one side after several moments. "Daniel?" she whispered.

"Yes?" Slowly, with infinite care, he brushed one fingertip against her lips, marveled at their silky fullness.

"Um—"

"Did you say something, Samantha?" She was unbearably lovely, her oval face pearly in the moonlight. Months of denial jumped overboard as he stared at her.

"Are you going to—"

"Yes, I am." Sliding his arms about her narrow waist, he drew her closer. "So if you're going to object you'd better do it now."

She said nothing, only looked at him as if she were seeing something for the first time. The temptation was too great. Daniel bent his head and kissed her as he'd longed to for what seemed an eternity.

After a moment Sam's arms slid around his neck and she leaned against him, returning his kiss with her own, deepening the embrace as her lips parted beneath his, asking—no, demanding—more.

In that moment Daniel forgot all about Finders, Inc., the mission and the ship. Everything. All that filled his brain was the pure, sweet knowledge that the woman he held in his arms apparently wanted to be there.

Sometime later he eased her away, He rested his chin against the top of her head while she leaned her cheek against his chest.

"Are you cold?" he asked against her earlobe.

"No." Her hands slid from his back, palms resting against his chest. "What are we doing, Daniel?"

"Kissing."

She drew in a quick breath of surprise then tapped his cheek. "I know that, silly. I was here. What I mean is, why?"

Because I've wanted to kiss you like that forever. Because you belong in my life. Because…

"Because this is paradise and you're very beautiful and we wanted to," he told her, staring over her head into the darkness. Because you fit in my arms like God put you there. Daniel gulped. He couldn't say that.

"But, Daniel—we don't even like each other." She leaned back to get a better look at his face. "I mean, you think I'm an incompetent idiot who needs a protector."

"Do I think that?" He dipped his head to touch her lips again, then drew back just enough to follow the tiny pulse down her neck. "What do you think?"

"I think—" She drew in a quick breath, shivered, pulled back. "I think I like that too much. And I can't. I've got a job to do."

"I'm not stopping you from doing it." He slid off his jacket, wrapped it around her shoulders. "But at the moment there's no one to chase, no one to spy on, no one to avoid. You're a very lovely woman, Samantha. You take my breath away. But you're wrong."

"I am? About what?"

"Whom. About whom. Me." He tucked his hand under her chin and lifted it so she had to look at him. The time for truth had finally arrived and he wasn't going to blow it. "I don't think you're incompetent, Samantha."

"You don't?"

He shook his head. "No. I think you're strong and independent and one of the best operatives Finders, Inc. has on staff. I admire your courage and tenacity, the way you go after what you want, that you don't give up without a fight, the way you set your goals and then pursue them no matter how difficult."

"Wow!" She gulped, managing a weak grin. "Have I been misreading you!"

He cupped her face in his hands and held her bemused gaze with his.

"I would never work against you, Samantha, or try

to stop you from getting what you deserve and have worked so hard to achieve. If I seemed to do that, I apologize. I respect your work and the way you get it done."

"Th-thank you." She studied him for several minutes. "Before, when you asked me out, I mean. I thought it was because—"

"Because I was testing you, trying to find a weak spot?" Daniel nodded, winced. "Believe me, if I didn't know it before, I got that message the day you took this assignment. You made your opinion pretty clear."

"What else was I supposed to think?" Her glorious eyes were spitting sparks. "That evening was a little unorthodox."

"It was?" He didn't remember it that way.

"You were testing me as if we were at a shooting range, Daniel!"

"It wasn't a shooting range—it was a duck pond at the local fair—and I took you there because I hadn't been to one, ever." He raked a hand through his hair. "You seemed to want one of those big teddy bears and I wanted you to have one. I was just trying to help you get it."

"So when I didn't hit the bull's-eye, you went and got it yourself." She grinned, a cheeky smile lighting her eyes. "How much did you spend?"

"Eighty-five dollars." Astonishment filled her face. He felt like a fool. "I'm not very good with a water pistol."

"The local toy store sells them for twenty bucks, Daniel," she whispered. "You could have saved some money."

He shrugged. "I could have. But I wanted to get it for you myself." He saw her lips quiver. "Go ahead and laugh. My father would have skinned me alive for wasting eighty-five dollars on a stuffed bear."

"Oh, Daniel." She burst out laughing, then hugged him so tightly he was afraid to breathe. "This picture you're painting—you realize it makes you look like a real softie?"

He tightened his arms around her, content to hold her like this until she told him to get lost. "Don't let it get around."

"Nobody would believe me anyway." Sam burrowed against him, half-turned so she could stare out to sea. "This is nice." After a long time had passed she spoke. "What was your father like?"

Every muscle in his body stiffened. Daniel swallowed hard and tried to think of something funny to say, but there was nothing funny about his father.

"Come on," she whispered. "Tell me."

"Domineering. Angry most of the time. Vindictive. Money was his idol." He clamped his mouth shut to stem the flow.

"But you loved him, right? And he loved you."

He could not answer truthfully so he remained silent; loath to shatter her idyllic world.

"I'm sure he did." She sighed, her breath brushing against his skin like feather down. "My father was gone a lot of the time, too. He worked two jobs, sometimes three to make ends meet, to get things for us. He thought that would prove how much he cared, but he didn't have to prove it. We knew." She drew away from him to stand by the rail, her fingers tight around it. "We always knew," she told him, her voice cracking.

"You were lucky."

"Was I?" She turned her head to face him and it was then he saw the tears cascading down her cheeks. "If he cared so much, then why did he kill himself? Can you explain that?"

"Oh, Samantha." He brushed the droplets from her skin with his thumbs, wishing he could see inside her head, understand how to ease her pain.

"He pushed us so hard. 'Never settle for enough,' he'd say over and over. 'You've got to have money behind you to accomplish anything. Money makes the difference in this world,'" she half sobbed. After a moment she regained control on a hiccuped laugh. "See, we have something in common. My dad was obsessed with money, too, only he never had enough." She choked back a sob. "He died bankrupt."

"I'm so sorry." Why hadn't he known this? He'd read her file a thousand times and yet—Daniel tried to draw her into his arms but she resisted. What had changed? "I'm very sorry about your father, Samantha."

"Are you?" She drew a deep breath, dashed away the tears then slid out of his jacket. "Here, I don't need this. I'm going back to the cabin."

When he caught up with her, he grasped her arm. "Wait a minute. I'll go with you."

"I don't need a protector!"

"I was thinking more as a friend, but either way, I'm going." He endured the glare, wondering how this tropical paradise had turned to winter so fast. "Lead on. I'll be right behind you."

"Leave me alone, Daniel," she demanded, her eyes flashing a warning. "Don't try to charm me or flatter me or kiss me again. We're here to do a job. That's all."

"Fine."

She blinked at his easy consent. "This can't happen again. I won't allow it. I'm only here to get that statue."

He opened his mouth like a fish gulping water, but

nothing came out. Not that it mattered. Sam had already turned on her heel and disappeared.

Something had changed. She was deliberately pushing him away, ignoring the sparks that had flown between them, and he wanted to know why.

An answer dawned. In all his dreams he'd never envisioned it, which was pretty stupid, considering her beauty.

Could it be that Sam wasn't interested in him because she wanted someone else. Someone like her friend Ric.

That thought sent chills up his spine.

SEVEN

"Samantha, it's breakfast time. How long will it take you to get ready?"

With a groan, she rolled over, stared at the clock. Nine-thirty? Why hadn't Daniel called her earlier?

"Sam?"

"Ten minutes," she yelled, heading for the bathroom.

It was more like thirty, but Daniel never said a word. In fact he maintained the same silence she'd endured yesterday. Aside from odd sideways glances and a few necessary questions, they'd spent the previous day sight-seeing. Dinner had been an equally quiet affair since Sanchez and his wife had not appeared.

After the closeness they'd shared on deck, Daniel's cool attitude confirmed for Sam that his kisses were the result of propinquity and her green dress. Daniel seemed able to easily dismiss those moments, yet she couldn't get them out of her mind. He was behaving nothing like the Daniel she thought she knew.

Sam took extra pains dressing then mocked herself for it. Why did she care what he thought of her? She was here to do a job. But no one could fault her on playing her part. The white sundress with its crisscross top and scooped-out back boosted her self-confidence. The sandals added height. She'd debated wearing them—for about twenty seconds. They were definitely not her style and she didn't remember choosing them so Daniel must have. Good choice. There were light, elegant and showed off her newly polished toenails.

The difference good clothes made amazed her. Of course, Daniel fit in here as easily as he did everywhere. No doubt years of private schools hobnobbing with the rich did that for you. But Sam had been worried about carrying this off. These clothes helped because they made her feel like someone else—maybe that's why she'd kissed him back. But it didn't explain the sweet pleasure she'd found in his arms or the fear she felt at her own response.

She tousled her hair, decided to let it dry naturally. A dab of mascara, some tinted lip gloss and she was ready.

"We've already anchored," he told her as they walked to the dining room. His attention rested on the gold coin she'd deliberately worn on her wrist. "You look—"

"Don't bother saying another word, Daniel. It's our only clue and I'm going to use it until the next one comes along." She prepared to defend her plan and was surprised by his smile.

"—lovely." He finished quietly.

"Oh. Sorry," she mumbled.

"I am not the bad guy here, Samantha."

He was right. It wasn't Daniel who was the bad guy, it was his father Howard, and because of that she didn't trust the son. That was probably wrong of her but lessons of the past were hard to forget and she had good reason to think poorly of McCullough Senior.

"I hope someday you can explain it to me so I can

fix whatever I did to spoil things," he said quietly, before the server showed them to their table.

"Just let it go," she begged.

They ate their meal in relative silence while the ship's speaker announced plans for disembarkation to visit Espinoza Point on Fernandina Island.

"A lot more birds, penguins and sea lions, apparently." Daniel sipped his coffee. "After lunch we go to Tagus Cove on Isabela Island. You can take scuba-diving lessons there if you want."

"Really?" She stared at him, enchanted by the thought of staying under the water with the fish, which was strange given her claustrophobia. Then she remembered. "What about sharks?"

"You'll be with a group. They won't bother you. Sharks prefer to be left alone." Daniel reached across the table to grasp her hand. "Our friends have arrived."

They greeted the Peruvian couple, but Daniel made no effort to include Señor Sanchez or his wife at their table or in any conversation, which was fine with Sam. She found it hard to breathe normally when his hand touched her. Guilt swelled. She'd let him believe he'd done something wrong when the fault lay with her and her roller-coaster emotions.

Sam didn't know exactly when it had happened, but something in her heart had changed toward him. The ogre she'd insulted that day at Finders was a figment of her imagination. The real Daniel was kind, generous, funny.

But he couldn't be more than that. Not to her.

"I can't help wondering why Sanchez is on this trip," Daniel muttered. "If he is Varga's boss, then the statue is already his and he doesn't have to wait for the auction."

"Patience, master. He'll show his hand sooner or

later." Sam bit into the succulent mango, relishing the piquant juice as it slid down her throat. "It could be it's his anniversary. Got any plans for today?"

"Isabela Island, which is the largest island in the Galapagos. I'm particularly interested in seeing the giant tortoises." He went on to describe what he'd learned. "I wonder where Varga is."

Three cups of coffee later, Sam was more than willing to get moving. If she didn't know better, she would have said Daniel was stalling. "Do I need to change before we go ashore?"

He did a slow assessment of her, bringing a blush to her cheeks. Finally his focus rested on her shoes. "Can you walk in those?"

"Of course. They're quite comfortable."

"They don't look like walking shoes." *Skeptical* didn't begin to describe his tone.

The sandals made her feel elegant. Sam was loath to take them off, so she did walk on Fernandina Island in them, right beside the Sally Lightfoot crabs and a colony of marine iguanas. If she stumbled a little, Daniel didn't seem to mind offering her his arm. He scouted out the best volcanic location from which to watch the penguins, hawks and sea lions, not to mention anyone who came ashore. He seemed in no hurry to leave as he surveyed God's creation.

Parched from the sun's heat, Sam twisted around to get the water bottle from her bag and promptly dropped it, gaping. "Do you see what I see? Over by the landing spot."

Daniel slid his arm around her shoulder and pretended he was helping her get more comfortable. In the process, he shifted enough to take a good look.

"Our Mr. Sanchez."

"With Varga and someone else."

"Yes." He leaned closer. "I wish I knew who the third is. Any ideas?"

"Could be the man who shoved us into the smoke." Daniel's touch was making her stomach do strange things. Sam jumped to her feet. "Let's go back to the ship. I think it's time I started asking some questions of my own."

"Wait. Sanchez is coming over here." Daniel slid tinted shields over his glasses before he drew her close, facing the ocean. "Relax," he whispered.

She didn't dare.

"Such a lovely sight."

"Hello there. We've been admiring the view." Daniel shifted, pointed behind him. "Do you think those lava flows are fairly recent?"

"I know little of the islands' history." It was clear Sanchez wanted something. He made no effort to move on.

"But you're from Lima—at least that's what the maître d' said." Daniel sounded surprised. "I assumed you'd made this trip before. I noticed you speaking to someone—I don't think they were on the ship."

"No. Another tourist, like us." Sanchez smiled. "I do travel for the museum, but I've never been here before. You will agree there's little here that would show well under glass in a museum."

"Maybe there's hidden treasure nearby." Sam yawned. His gaze rested on her wrist. She moved it deliberately so the light caught the gold.

Daniel's grip on her waist tightened. "That reminds me, I've heard many stories of buried treasure near your country, Señor Sanchez. My father was obsessed with

such tales. In fact, we often came down to search for it when I was a child."

"Indeed." Sanchez rocked back on his heels, his white shirt and pants brilliant in the sun. His eyes remained half-closed, unreadable. "Your father—did he find this treasure he sought?"

"Sadly no. He died before his dream came true."

"Too bad. But of course any treasure found in Peruvian waters would be the property of our government. It is a matter of international law." Sanchez shaded his eyes. "Sometimes treasure seekers forget such details."

A muscle in Daniel's cheek flicked and Sam knew he was tired of their verbal fencing. She'd try the more direct approach.

"But if treasure is found in international waters, that's not the same as something that has been stolen from someone and transported into a country illegally, is it?"

"Indeed, no. Not the same at all." Sanchez's eyes narrowed. "Is that how you came by your bracelet, Ms. Henderson?"

"Oh, I'm not a treasure hunter or a thief." She held up her arm. "This was a gift. From a friend. Didn't I tell you that?" She felt the warning pressure from Daniel's fingers, translating it to mean "be careful."

"The friend who gave you this gift—perhaps he has more of such things?"

"If he did they're probably gone." She met his stare. "He's dead now. Someone killed him. I saw it happen."

"*¡Ah Dios!*" Señor Sanchez froze. His face tightened until it looked as if it were carved from stone. Time hung suspended while he searched her face. "A terrible thing," he squeaked. "Such a tragedy when friends die."

"Especially when they didn't have to. And I don't

think God had anything to do with it." She refused to back down.

"God has to do with everything, *chiquita.* We can never forget that He watches us always." When he summoned a smile, he lost the grave tone. "Death makes us appreciate life all the more, no?"

Sam opened her mouth to give him her opinion, but Daniel spoke first.

"Say, you are a curator of a museum, is that correct?"

"*Sí.* The Inca Museum in Lima."

"Then perhaps you can tell us something about the coin." Daniel held up Sam's wrist to offer him a look. "Other than that it's from Spain, I mean."

Sanchez seemed unconcerned they'd take his actions for greed as he grasped the metal disk. His other hand held Sam's wrist immovable.

"Be careful," Sam murmured. "It's a delicate chain. I wouldn't want to lose my friend's gift. It's the only thing I have to remember him by."

"Of course, Ms. Henderson. Very careful." He leaned closer as he examined back and front in a detailed minute search. "Sixteen eighty-nine," he whispered. "It is very old."

"Well, we already knew that." Sam tugged her hand free of his damp grip. "Daniel thinks it came off a ship—what was it called? The *Carolina?*"

"Close, honey."

Sam pressed on despite the censure she heard in his voice.

"There were supposed to be gold chests on board," she ad-libbed. "Money from Spain to buy land or something. I forget how the story went."

"I know nothing of this ship. I must check our records." Sanchez stroked a hand against his jaw, but his focus returned to her wrist. "There are many who would pay well for such a coin to add to their collection."

"Really. Like who?" She turned to Daniel. "Maybe I should sell it."

"Of course, you'd be paid substantially more if you could add to the collection, *señorita.*"

"Really? How many would make a collection?" Sam kept her eyes on Sanchez, ignoring Daniel's swift intake of breath. They needed something to go on. "How much could I get if I had, say, a hundred coins?"

Sanchez almost choked. "Your, er, friend had that many coins?"

"Maybe more. I'm not sure."

"Samantha, we—"

"Wait!" The Peruvian's eyes glittered with greed. "I'm sure I, through the museum, of course, could guarantee that you would receive enough to live very handsomely from such a sale. Or I can arrange to find a buyer if you prefer that. Shall I begin the search?"

"Samantha was speaking hypothetically. She doesn't have any more coins at the moment." Daniel grasped her elbow. "You look warm, *dear.* Perhaps we should go back to the ship."

"It is true, *señorita?*" Sanchez dabbed his handkerchief against his brow. "You do not have any more coins?"

"Not yet, but maybe I can find some more." She smiled at Daniel. "You're right. I do feel hot."

"The sun is very strong. We'll no doubt see you later, Señor Sanchez." He led Sam off the lava and onto the path. "You look a bit flushed, darling," he said as his arm slid around her waist.

Well, who wouldn't be flushed? Daniel was hanging

on to her as if he couldn't bear to let her go. His touch affected her heart rate and the muscles in her legs. She had to endure silently as Sanchez chose to walk with them, smiling beneficently as if he alone were responsible for the gorgeous day.

"Your wife isn't visiting the island today?" Sam watched his face.

"I regret my wife is not as fond of nature as I." He didn't look worried by that, more relieved.

"That's too bad. The Galapagos Islands are among the very best examples of nature untouched." Obviously Daniel wondered why the woman had even come on such a trip. "Is she not well?"

"She is fine," Sanchez snapped.

"Now, Daniel, not all of us dream of traveling up the Amazon." Sam edged away from his fingers at her waist.

"I was thinking about that very thing for our next trip." Daniel glanced at Sanchez. "Iquitos, isn't that where the Amazon begins? I read of a wonderful tour there. Do you know anything about that, *señor?*"

"No. I seldom go into the country." He paused at the bottom of the ramp that led inside the ship. "If you find the coins, *señorita,* or if you get any more, you will give me first opportunity, won't you?"

"Oh. I suppose I could. At least, I'll try. Say hello to your wife for me."

"Yes." Sanchez remained behind, watching. Daniel's hand returned to her waist as they walked up the stairs to their cabin.

Once inside, she turned on him. "Will you please let go of me?" she hissed. "I'm not an invalid."

"Sorry." He held up his hands while backing away. "Just trying to keep up the illusion of a loving couple."

Any woman in her right mind would have begged a man like Daniel McCullough to continue that illusion. They'd probably have hoped and dreamed he'd kiss them again, too.

Which begged the question—was Sam in her right mind for turning him away? The indecision was hers alone. Daniel's confidence went unquestioned. Cookie-cutter handsome with that chiseled jaw, hollows under his cheekbones and the merest hint of five-o'clock shadow at noon—Daniel didn't need to prove a thing. Once she'd thought his glasses an affectation, but now that she knew he needed them they'd become part of who Daniel was, faint barriers he sometimes used as a shield.

In the loose yet elegant clothes, with those dark lenses shielding his thoughts, this Daniel looked totally different from the quiet, complacent man she'd known at Finders, Inc. An edge of mystery surrounded him and intrigued her so much that Samantha caught herself cataloguing each nuance in his actions and voice, hoping it would help her understand him better.

She'd heard stories about the many disguises he'd assumed and carried off with such aplomb. The past few days helped Samantha believe it. For a few moments on deck that night she'd felt utterly cherished, tenderly shielded and completely treasured. But that was an act, wasn't it?

"Sam?" He touched her arm, his concern evident.

"Yes?"

"I asked what you were doing—all the talk about coins and treasure. Are you trying to get yourself hurt?"

"No." She bristled at the censure. "I'm trying to figure out if he's the one who's after the coins or simply a go-between. Judging by his offer, I'd say he's acting on his own, but he said he knows a man. Maybe he means Obrigado. He's well-known for his love of all things gold." She sat down to think it through. "I'm almost certain Sanchez didn't know about the coins before he came on board. He didn't bat an eye when you mentioned Iquitos or the Amazon."

"He sure did flinch when you said Bert had died. I wonder if that means he knew him. Or of him?"

"I don't know. You don't think Sanchez is working on his own, do you?" She'd already made up her mind, but she wanted his take.

"No. He was talking to Varga for quite a while. I'd say they're acquainted. I think the third guy was giving them information, maybe about the statue. My guess is Sanchez is getting ready to make his own deal."

"I wonder why we haven't seen Obrigado yet. It's a big ship, but still you'd think we'd have caught a glimpse." She blinked as an idea emerged. "Maybe that's who Sanchez was talking to on the beach. I didn't get a close enough look to be sure."

"You'd have to ID him. I don't know the guy." Daniel rubbed the nape of his neck. "I gather neither Sanchez nor Obrigado are el Zopilote?"

She shook her head.

"So we're still missing someone. I'd like to know who the guy who locked us in that room is working for."

"I'm pretty sure Varga's boss is this el Señor. Obrigado has connections, but he's always been on his own. That leaves Sanchez, and I think he'd make whatever deal he could to get the statue." Samantha looked around for her phone. "I'm going to do some checking on the other guests that were on that list

Finders sent me. Maybe something will come up that we hadn't thought of. Can I borrow your laptop?"

"Sure." Daniel watched her slide off her sandals. "You're a strange combination, Samantha." He removed his sunglasses and blinked with that wise-owl stare that probed too deep.

"I don't know what you mean."

"You deliberately placed yourself in unknown danger to find out about the coins, but you won't let anyone get close enough to see the real you."

"This is the real me, Daniel." She refused to let him get to her. "My job defines who I am."

"I think it's a cover you use so no one will see past it to the real Sam."

She froze then shrugged. "Think what you like, but this pretense of ours isn't fooling anyone."

"We don't know that—yet." He interrupted her protest. "I'm not going to force you, Samantha. This is your case. If you want to drop the charade right now, we will. But I believe we'll get better results if people perceive us as a team. Otherwise we have no real excuse to be on this particular cruise and that makes us stand out."

"I don't like lying." She booted up his computer.

"They're drawing their own conclusions from the way we act." He waited, enduring her glare. "If you don't like it, if you want to change things, you can talk to me, you know. There's no need for pretense, Sam."

"Are you kidding me?" She waved a hand around the room. "Pretense is exactly what all this is about."

"I meant here in this room, between us. I'm not here to judge you or coerce you, but it would help if you could trust me not to pounce every time I touch you or ask a question."

"I'm...sorry. I'm just not used to it." She didn't look at him for fear he'd see the truth. "That's why I work on my own."

"And that's why I was concerned about moving you into the supervisor job. You put up a protective barrier and that doesn't make for good teamwork." He continued before she could protest. "Have some faith in me, Samantha. I'm not out to ruin your operation. I'm just here to help."

He walked to his door and pushed it open.

"What are you doing now?"

"There's enough time to check with the office before lunch. Maybe they've got something new to tell us." He closed the panel behind him with a quiet finality.

Sam bit her lip. The truth hurt, but this stung. She didn't get the job and not because he was putting her down or denying her something she could handle. He'd refused the promotion because she was a loner, because she hadn't shown cooperation as one of her strengths. He was right. She preferred working alone, because she knew she could depend on herself. She wasn't so sure about everyone else.

Daniel couldn't know that she needed that barrier between them, that she couldn't allow herself to lean on him, let him take charge, because she was afraid he'd do exactly what his father had done—ruin everything.

She'd set the ground rules; he'd followed her lead. Daniel didn't fight, wouldn't argue with her or force her to do things his way. He wouldn't even rise to her baiting. It looked as though he was totally focused on the mission.

"A lesson you'd do well to learn," she reminded herself. She got to work on his laptop, pausing when a knock at the door disturbed her thoughts.

"Message for Ms. Henderson."

Daniel emerged from his room, watching as Sam opened the door.

"I'm Samantha Henderson." She accepted the single rose and the white envelope from the uniformed man. "Thank you."

She laid the rose on the table, slit the envelope and slid out the single piece of paper, aware that Daniel never moved.

"There's no signature, but I think it's from Ric. He sent me a rose once before with a message." Heat burned her cheeks as she read the words. "He wants me to meet him on the Starlight deck tonight at midnight—to talk about the statue." She held it out. "Do you want to read it?"

Daniel studied the note, his face impassive. He shrugged. "Not much to go on here, but Finders hasn't anything, either. No word of the statue anywhere. It's like it disappeared into a hole."

"Or into a museum in Lima," she said, giving him an arch look.

"There's that." He blinked as if he was sleepy. "Are you ready for lunch? We could go anytime now."

"As soon as I find another pair of shoes."

He picked up one of her white sandals by the strap. "You don't like these?"

"Yes, but you were right." He raised an eyebrow and she hurried on. "I shouldn't have worn them around Fernandina Island." She offered him a tentative smile, a sort of truce.

"Feet hurt, huh?" Daniel dropped the shoe, walked to the door and waited for her to join him.

"Can we skip the dining room today?" she asked as

they left the suite. "I'd like to eat on deck in the fresh air, away from the scrutiny of that Sanchez man. I want something light and refreshing—a salad maybe."

"As you wish." He found them a table at the café beside the deck railing. He waited while she chose her lunch from the menu, then asked for his usual omelet.

"You've had that several times. Is there something special in it that I should know about?" she asked when their food arrived.

Daniel was in the act of sipping iced tea from his glass. He looked at the omelet oozing cheese, onions, green and jalapeño peppers and a host of other vegetables, and he compared it with her choice. "Would you like to trade?"

"No, thanks. Too spicy for me." She picked up her fork to dig into her chicken salad. "This is more my style."

"Uh-huh." He leaned back in his chair and studied her. "You hardly look like plain old chicken salad, Samantha."

"In spite of the fancy clothes, I'm the same as I always was, though this cruise is good for making a person feel pampered." She squeezed the wedge of lemon over the salad and licked her lips.

"Don't you like it?"

"I love this salad." He made a face and she giggled. "Oh, you mean pampering?" She wrinkled her nose and then nodded. "It's fine for a while, I guess. But I don't think I'd ever make it as one of the idle rich. Not that I'm ever likely to find out." If she didn't get some results here, and fast, she'd probably be looking for another job. "You, on the other hand, look like you were born to live the high life."

He seemed startled. "Why do you say that?"

"I don't know. A certain je ne sais quoi, I suppose. It

isn't obvious or anything. It's more that you seem completely comfortable among the diamonds and fancy clothes that are part of this scene. Something you learned at one of those fancy prep schools?" She bit her lip, realizing she'd given away her secret—that she knew about his past.

"Nope. I left before they taught that."

"How do you do it then?"

One finger crooked, beckoning her forward across the table. He leaned in until his face was bare inches away. His eyes sparkled with topaz lights she hadn't noticed before. "I fake it."

"Pardon?"

"I pretend I'm playing a part, that the tux or tails is part of my disguise. My character is Sir Jefferson Pattersby and he comes from the very elite among noblemen." He grinned. "Works every time."

Slightly shocked by the change in him, Sam could only stare until a sharp spasm grabbed her stomach and shot waves of nerve-tightening pain to her face. "Oh!"

He was beside her in an instant. "What's wrong?"

"Allergy," she managed to sputter, though her jaws felt as if iron bands had gripped them.

"To chicken?"

She shook her head. Daniel leaned forward and poked through her salad. At the bottom lay a bit of something that was not chicken. His face tightened. "Crabmeat, I'm guessing. Do you have an Epi pen?"

She tried to nod. "Room," she gasped as the pressure on her chest increased.

"Let's go." He grabbed her hand, and pulled her across the deck. When she stumbled, he lifted her into his arms. A waiter came hurrying over. "Someone put shellfish in her salad and she's allergic," she heard him say. "I've got to get her to our room."

The man yelled to someone else who came running. Between them, they cleared the halls and grabbed the first elevator. To Sam it seemed to take forever as she tried to get breath into her lungs. She could hear herself wheezing as the door opened.

"Get the doctor," Daniel ordered the two men. "Where's the pen, Sam?" he demanded, laying her carefully on the bed.

"Second drawer." A moment later he'd plunged the needle in her arm. Eventually the pain began to ease off her chest and she could breathe easier.

When at last the world returned to normal, Daniel was hovering over the bed. A cool cloth wiped her forehead and lips. Then he offered her some water, his smile reassuring, gentle.

"Relax. The doctor's here. He wants to take a look at you."

"I'm fine." But she was powerless to stop the white-suited man from gently examining her. Some time later a soft blanket covered her. "Daniel?"

"Yes, it's me. You need to rest now, get your strength back. I'll be around, don't worry. You take it easy."

"But the island," she whispered as a rush of tears rose unbidden. "You'll miss seeing the turtles."

"There will be plenty of turtles on the next island. Or we'll come back. It doesn't matter. The important thing is you're okay." He pushed the hair away from her face, his fingers gentle, tender. "Don't fuss about it."

His hand touched hers and she grabbed on to it like a lifeline, heaving a sigh of relief.

"Thanks for not bawling me out. I couldn't have

taken that." As she pressed her head back into the pillow, she closed her eyes. "Daniel?"

"Yes, Samantha?"

"Do you think it was an accident?"

EIGHT

An accident?

Sure. And he believed in the tooth fairy and Santa Claus, too.

Daniel watched Samantha sleep for another moment then closed the door, her words ringing in his ears. *Thanks for not bawling me out.* Is that how she thought of him—as some kind of judgmental taskmaster?

He grabbed the phone and demanded the purser's office. He learned the kitchen was aware of her allergy and had taken special pains to ensure no seafood was in it.

"We do, however, have some new kitchen help and it is possible that one of them mixed up an order."

"This wasn't a mix-up. The crab was buried at the bottom." He wasn't helping. "I'd like the names of whoever was working at the time."

"I'm sorry. We do not give out the names of our employees. But you may be certain we are doing everything we can so this doesn't happen again."

Daniel thought a moment. "Okay, but tell me, was a man named Varga on duty at the time?"

There was a slight hesitation, then the sound of

papers shuffling. “We do not have anyone by that name on staff, Mr. McCullough.”

With no other options, Daniel hung up. As soon as he did, the phone rang. He grabbed it, hoping it wouldn’t wake Sam. Before he could say anything, a voice spoke.

“Be at Tagus Cove, by the graffiti at 3:45 if you want to know about the statue.”

Two and a half hours until the meeting date. Daniel didn’t dare leave Sam for fear someone would try to hurt her again, and perhaps succeed this time. But finding the statue was her mission and he didn’t want to see her fail. There had to be some way he could get there without leaving her alone. He called to enquire, but since the cruise had no children aboard there were no sitters available. Off-duty staff were visiting the island.

Minutes crawled past like snails—every moment torture as he waited for the appointed hour and knew he’d have to miss this chance to find out more. He checked his messages from Finders, Inc. Shelby had learned that Señor Sanchez had recently withdrawn a large sum of money from his personal account—for a statue?

“Daniel?”

“I’m here.” After walking into Sam’s room, he studied her pale face, the way she struggled to sit upright. “How are you feeling?”

“I’m fine. Just lazy.” She leaned back against the pillows and searched his face. “What’s wrong?”

“Nothing.”

“That’s a lie. You said we’d have the truth between us.”

“Yes I did.” He told her about the phone call. “Any ideas?”

“No.” She glanced at his watch. “But we’ve only got an hour left! Why didn’t you wake me?”

"You're not going anywhere," he exclaimed. As she rose from the bed, she teetered slightly before regaining her balance. "Look at you! You can hardly stand up straight. You're in no shape—"

She turned on him, her eyes hard and glittering.

"This is my case, Daniel. I'll decide what I can and can't do. Right now I'm going to Tagus Cove to meet whoever phoned and find out exactly what he knows. Now please leave me alone. I'm going to do this on my own."

There was no point in arguing, but Daniel was determined Sam would not meet this nebulous informant unprotected. With the strict security measures imposed on the ship, he'd had no way to get a weapon aboard—meaning that as a bodyguard he'd be almost defenseless. The only thing he could do was pray for heavenly protection and stand in front of her if need be.

When Sam emerged from her room dressed in slim navy shorts and a white blouse, she gave him only the most cursory glance.

"I'm going, too," he told her as she tied on a pair of navy-and-white sneakers. "Don't bother to argue."

"You're the boss," she murmured, her hair shielding her face from him. "Who am I to argue? Just stay out of my way."

"I'm not going as your boss. I'm going as your partner, as your friend, as a second set of eyes. Once we get on land I'll change into somebody else," he promised. "You won't even know I'm there."

Her eyes expressed her doubts, but Sam didn't say anything, merely grabbed her straw bag and pulled open the door. As they passed the gift shop, Sam stopped to ask about the auction to be held. Daniel used the opportunity to sneak a uniform off a rack of laundry. He stuffed it inside his bag. It wasn't stealing. He'd return it later.

"There's just one thing," he added as they waited to go through the security check. "Stay in the open. As far as I could find out, the graffiti is supposed to be written on a rock cliff so that shouldn't be a problem. Just don't go into any caves."

She waited until they were on dry land before letting her sunglasses drop to the end of her nose so she could glare over them.

"I've been doing this long enough to know the tricks of the trade. And I do not need a nursemaid."

"Cooperation. Remember, Samantha?"

She sauntered away from him, following a tour guide toward the lava flows.

"Ah, an argument in paradise?" Sanchez appeared beside Daniel, his eyes narrowed as Sam disappeared into a crowd. "May I offer some advice from an old married man? Sometimes it is more peaceful to let them think they know best, *señor.*"

"Thanks." Like he needed advice from this guy. Still, the opportunity had presented itself and Daniel wasn't about to let it go. "*Señor,* you offered to find a buyer for those coins. Are you able to procure items for sale also?"

"Such as?"

"Samantha is particularly interested in a certain sculpture. I'd really like to get it for her." Boldness couldn't hurt at this point.

"A sculpture?"

"More like a statue, really. She read about it. Some fellow had it in his collection and decided to give it to a museum, except it never arrived." He kept his eyes trained on Sam. "I thought maybe I could find something like that."

"I see." Sanchez gave nothing away. "Well, without some specific information I cannot tell you much. Do you have a picture of this statue?"

"Hmm." Daniel scratched his head, senses clicking to high alert as a person approached Samantha. He told himself to calm down when the fellow walked away after a moment. "I might be able to get one."

"While we're on the ship?" Sanchez shot back, black eyes glowing as if he'd just trapped his prey.

"Oh, yeah." Daniel laughed at his own foolishness. "I wonder if the ship would allow me to receive a fax. Maybe we could stop by your museum when the cruise is over. I have a friend who could send me information about the statue. Then you'd have something to go on."

"That is a possibility, *señor*. Let us mull on this further." Sanchez flashed his fake smile again. "Now, please excuse me. I want to see the cliffs and the so-famous saltwater lagoon of Darwin and there is not much time left."

"Certainly." Daniel deliberately slowed his steps, hanging back as most of the others pressed forward. Sam was still with the group, climbing the hill now toward a rocky cliff. A cabana for those who wished to change from their bathing clothes stood not five feet from him. Perfect.

Daniel emerged in the uniform he'd filched. He pulled the cap firmly down, shading his eyes. His sunglasses added extra protection. After a quick scour, he joined the tail end of a group whose tour guide had just began her spiel.

"Isabela Island is the largest island in the Galapagos

and was created by the eruption of five volcanoes that flowed together. The graffiti we are going to see dates back to the 1800s and is believed to have been done by pirates and buccaneers."

Daniel eased his way past the group and lengthened his stride to more quickly cover the ground. Samantha stood staring at the rocks as if she were searching for something very important.

It was three-forty. Five minutes until the meet. When he was within a few hundred feet of Sam, Daniel slowed up, pretending to study the rocks.

"I suppose you do this route so often, you get tired of the tourist sites." A man in the park's khaki uniform stood next to him.

Daniel faked an English accent, but didn't turn his head. "Always something spectacular on these islands, mate."

"That's true." The man hung around for a few minutes more, then pointed. "I just started this job and I always get turned around. Is that the way to the dinghies?"

Daniel chuckled as if truly amused. "You've got me. Can't stand little boats. Avoid them like the plague, if you catch my drift." He plucked at his white shirt with the insignia of the cruise line then hooted with laughter.

"Oh. Yeah. Very funny. Little boats." The guy smiled but his whole demeanor projected a certain tenseness. "Thanks anyway." He turned away.

But not soon enough. The khaki hat tipped back just enough to offer a full view of his face.

Daniel knew him! He didn't know how or why—not yet, anyway. But he'd seen this guy before, he was certain of it. He half turned and watched the man walk away from him, pause beside Sam, touch her arm. His back blocked her face, but Daniel had the distinct impression that Sam was glad to see him. They talked for several moments before the man grabbed her arm and drew her away from the cliffs. He shook his head at something she said, leaned down to kiss her cheek, then hurried away, soon disappearing behind a lava formation that concealed whatever lay beyond.

Daniel followed Sam at a safe distance. He kept her in sight until he spotted a location mostly hidden from the view of those staring at the rocks. Thus protected, he changed back into his own clothes then stuffed the uniform into his backpack. He got back to the lagoon just in time to see Sam board one of the dinghies for the ride to see more wildlife.

He had to stand in line for the next one and it was more than half an hour before he caught up to her at the boarding entrance.

"Where have you been?" she asked once they'd passed the security checkpoint and were climbing the stairs to their deck.

"Around. Who was the guy you met with? And don't tell me he works here. He doesn't."

She tipped her head back to stare at him. "You saw?"

"I told you I wouldn't be far away." He waited.

"So the rumors about your disguise capability were true." She grimaced. "I didn't even notice you. Anyway, that was Ric. He had some news about the statue." She unlocked the room, went inside. Daniel followed. "I told you about Ric, remember?"

Boy did he remember. "Your CIA friend. I thought he was meeting you tonight."

"Ex-CIA." She frowned. "I forgot to ask him about that."

"How did he get here?"

"I didn't ask and Ric didn't explain. Is it important?" She raised one eyebrow.

"I don't know. Go on."

"According to the transit documents, the statue was never supposed to be part of the Inca Museum's inventory. But Ric's pretty sure Sanchez used his museum's connections to buy the statue for his country hoping he could slide it into his personal collection."

"Where is it now?"

"That's the thing. Ric thinks Varga was supposed to transport it to the Sanchez house but never showed up. Ric thinks Varga got a better offer. Maybe that's what they were discussing on the beach yesterday."

"Better offer from whom?"

Her brow creased. "Ric didn't say. His feeling is Varga's got some prearranged signal at the auction for the buyer to know."

Hadn't she told him Ric was working on another case? So how and why had he come by this information? "What is your friend doing here? It's a fairly isolated area to just happen by."

"He's tracking drugs."

"On our particular ship?" he asked curiously, wondering how far she was prepared to let coincidence go.

"I don't think so. At least he isn't on our cruise, because he said a friend relayed his message."

"Oh." So he wasn't on board. Something to be thankful for. Daniel decided that when they got back he'd hound Shelby again for more information on Sam's elusive Ric.

"He asked me about my coin. I hope you didn't mind that I told him about your uncle."

He did mind, but Daniel couldn't explain why.

Neither did he intend to tell her he'd seen Ric before, not until he'd figured out where. "I guess we might as well get ready for dinner."

"What about later?"

"Later?" Daniel noticed Sam had a wan, weary look that told him she needed rest, not more worry.

"The note. The top deck, remember? About the statue."

"Right." He thought a moment. "If Ric didn't send it, who did?"

"Good question. And why the rose?" She tapped one finger against her cheek. "Does it seem smart that someone would put the crab in my salad, knowing I'd get sick, and still expect me to make it to the meeting?"

"Feels like a third party, someone who doesn't want you there, maybe wants the statue for himself. Or—who else knew about your allergy?"

"The kitchen. I made sure it was notified when we checked in for the cruise."

"You mentioned it the night we ate with Sanchez." He held her gaze. "Maybe the statue is up for sale and he wants you out of the way."

"How did he get access to my food?" She sighed. "Doesn't matter. I'll be there tonight for sure."

Daniel wasn't quite sure how to phrase his thoughts. "Your Ric is quite the fount of information, isn't he?"

"He's not my Ric, but yes, I think he's very good at his job." She glared at him. "Why do you resent his success, Daniel?"

"Pardon?" Where had this come from?

"It's clear you don't like Ric. You even had him researched. And I know you've got a tally sheet on me, how many cases I solved, how many I let go, stuff like that."

"That's what I do, Sam. Analysis for Finders, Inc."

"Sure it is. Only you analyze everyone. All the time. We all have to jump up to your standard, don't we, Daniel? I think you're more like your father than you know."

"Meaning?" He hated the implication, hated it even more that she put him and his father in the same breath. If she only understood how hard he'd worked *not* to be like him.

"I've read every article I could find on Howard McCullough. Most of them said the same thing. In the end he didn't trust anyone. Not his researchers, not his friends, not his colleagues. He had paid spies in his company, suspected everyone. Why was he so suspicious?" She kept her eyes trained on him. "I think he was afraid."

"Afraid?" He wanted to yell at her to stop, but instead Daniel took a seat and waited, tense knots tying his stomach. "You keep harking back to my father. Why don't you tell me what interests you so much," he said quietly.

"Why? Because you're becoming like him. You talk about cooperation yet don't bother to share what you learned when you talked to Finders today." She sat down across from him, her face glowing with the passion that filled her voice. "It's not just me, either. You're constantly asking Finders for updates on other operations as if you're waiting for one of us to mess up."

"I'm doing my job."

"Ric isn't your job. He's my friend and he's been a great help. Why can't you accept that?"

Because Ric was too close to Sam and Daniel didn't like it.

"I'm doing the best I can on this case, Daniel, but I feel I can never live up to that impossible standard you've set."

"That is not true." He couldn't believe she'd said it, thought he was exactly what he'd striven not to become—a control freak. Just like dear old dad.

"Then act like it. This isn't my first mission. Okay, maybe I'm not always cooperative. I'll try harder. But you have to back off and let me do my job. Believe me when I say Ric isn't the bad guy. He's trying to help me. Because he's a *friend*."

"Apparently a very good one." Daniel wished he hadn't said it.

"Is that wrong?" She met his look and held it, her face pale. "You have a poster on your office wall, Strive For Perfection. It's a nice ideal, but it's not possible, Daniel. Mistakes are part of living."

"You could get burned." He felt bewildered, as if he'd met a cyclone.

"I'll recover. I do my job, but I won't allow myself to become so jaded I think everyone's out to get me."

"I never—"

"Your father did. From what I've read, he was paranoid that nobody could run his company as well as he did." She yanked off her sneakers as she spoke, her movements vigorous.

"I know exactly what my father was like, Samantha," he growled, hating the rush of guilt that burbled up inside. "I don't need you to remind me."

"Don't you? I think time has made you forget the things he did."

"What things?" There was something in her voice. "You sound like you knew him."

"Of course I didn't. What would I have in common with the great Howard McCullough?" But she didn't look at him.

"I don't know." He frowned at the rich red tide of color that washed her skin. Sam was hiding something. "Care to share?"

"I did do some research on him when you became CEO," she admitted.

Why would she have researched his father? Daniel let that go and concentrated on the present.

"Leaving my father out of it, you've obviously taken my concerns the wrong way. I'm glad you trust Ric, though realistically he didn't give us much we hadn't already surmised." He let that sink in, then continued, "I can't ignore my questions about him because he doesn't check out. Shelby can't find any record of him having been with the CIA." He held up his hand to stop her protest. "If he was working covertly, there should be someone who'd tell Finders to back off. No one's done that. I have to ask why."

"Fine. Forget Ric. He isn't the problem here anyway. You are." She drew open the bedroom door.

"Me?"

"You talk about trusting God. You want me to trust you, but you won't trust me enough to tell me what's at the bottom of your suspicions about Ric."

He kept silent. Sam shrugged and checked her watch.

"Here's what I know for sure. Someone is trying to lead us down the garden path about that statue, or maybe sidetrack us with the coins. I don't know why. But I intend to find out from whoever said they'll meet us at midnight. Right now I'm going to change for dinner."

Daniel entered his own room. But while he was dressing, the memory of her words returned. He felt more certain than ever that Samantha had a reason for researching his father, a reason she wasn't prepared to discuss. Yet.

Every instinct he possessed told him to bail before he became any more personally involved. But he couldn't bring himself to leave her here, alone, at the mercy of a man whose face his subconscious knew, a face that started the nerve in his neck thrumming a warning.

Ric Preston was a man who darted in and out of this investigation like a mosquito, supposedly on the trail of drugs. But there were none involved here. So why was Ric keeping tabs on their every move?

Because of Sam.

That was the scariest thought he'd had all day.

NINE

Samantha felt only relief that the meal was almost over. Though the tension between them was thick, to anyone watching, nothing had changed. Daniel was a good actor.

"The dinner show tonight is supposed to be interesting. Want to go?"

Since they had to wait another four hours till midnight, Sam nodded.

"Might as well," she agreed. "It's too wet to do anything on deck."

The steady drizzle echoed her mood. The cabin steward had assured her that the rain would be gone in a couple of hours but its dampening effect now made her wonder why she'd ever agreed to this assignment. So far all she seemed to do was run in circles.

"Shall we?" he asked as he rose, waited for her to precede him.

Always gracious, always polite. No one could fault his manners. By comparison, Sam felt mean and spoiled. What right did she have impugning his father? Even if Howard McCullough had been a jerk toward her father, Daniel didn't need to know that.

"Will you have a service for your uncle when we get back?" she asked as they waited for the curtain to go up.

"The mission society he worked with will have already arranged something. But I'd like to go back to the jungle where he worked, spend a few hours remembering him. I think he loved it there best anyway." He didn't look at her. "Maybe we can find that chest you saw."

"You haven't heard anything more about his killer?"

"No."

So whatever he and Shelby had discussed was still top secret. As the lights dimmed, Sam decided to sit back and let sleeping dogs lie. If Daniel wanted to talk to her, he'd talk.

The presentation was a type of variety show. A dance troupe presented a variation on *Swan Lake* that was particularly haunting. As they left the stage, a movement to the right drew Sam's attention. She grabbed Daniel's arm.

"Varga," she whispered.

He followed her stare, and then rose as the next number began. "Stay here. I'll be back."

He was gone before she could protest. A waiter passed with a tray of drinks. Sam chose a tropical juice concoction and sipped it as she kept watch. Where was he?

There was nothing to do but wait. But when the end of the show drew near, Sam could remain seated no longer. She slipped out before the rest of the crowd and was approaching the elevator to return to her room when a hand grasped her elbow.

"If you want to see your boyfriend alive, come with me." She recognized neither the face nor the voice, so it was sheer folly to obey, but the thought of Daniel lying unconscious in some closet overwhelmed her.

"Who are you? What do you want?" she asked, keeping her voice low as they walked along a corridor.

"El Señor wants what you took. Otherwise, you will die like the padre."

Sam swallowed hard. Daniel would never have come to this floor but she couldn't leave now. She needed answers.

"Is el Señor on the ship?"

A sneer. "You will meet him soon enough, *señorita,* if you do not return his merchandise."

She glanced around. They'd left most of the crowd behind and were now in an almost deserted corridor on a level few people used. One lone steward worked at the far end.

"Do you mean the statue?"

His reaction confirmed her suspicions. He looked confused. "El Señor does not want a silly statue. He wants what is his."

She needed time to sort this out. Sam jerked her arm out of his grasp. "Tell el Señor I don't have whatever it is he wants. And you stay away from me," she ordered in a louder tone. "If you bother me again, I'll alert security on the ship."

The attendant stopped, took a second look at her companion, who quickly turned away.

"You should not have done that," he hissed, his face glowering.

"Don't you threaten me, buddy." She planted herself in his path and visually dared him to move. "You tell el Señor to stop playing games. If he wants to talk to me he knows where to find me. It's not going to do him any good to threaten me, so he might as well forget it. I'm not interested in skulking around. Whatever he wants, he can ask me himself." She pointed upward at the security camera. "By now you should be pretty identifiable on tape."

"This is a mistake."

"It sure is." She turned to the attendant. "Will you please report this man to the captain? I never expected to endure such treatment on a cruise like this."

As the attendant moved forward, Samantha turned and climbed the stairs to her deck then moved quickly down the aisle with only a couple of glances over her shoulder. Once inside the room, she closed the door and double-locked it, then sat down in a chair while her heart rate returned to normal.

The man who'd ordered Bert's death was not el Zopilote. The man she'd seen was called el Señor and he thought she had something. So who was el Zopilote? If she could just find Varga, get him to answer some questions.

She checked her watch. Eleven-thirty. If she was going to make that rendezvous, there wasn't much time left.

With the gorgeous purple silk gown back on the hanger, Sam scrounged for something more appropriate for skulking around in the dark. At a quarter to twelve, she made her way up using the most traversed stairwells. Once outside, it was simply a matter of sticking to the shadows and hoping her black top and pants would provide enough cover. The rain had stopped, but the clouds offered plenty of cover.

She'd asked Daniel to let her handle things on her own, but she'd expected him to act as backup. Where was he?

Starlight deck at midnight. To talk about the statue.

"Well, here I am," she said to herself. "Where are you?"

"Right here." Varga held her shoulder, kept her from turning around.

"Not this again. I ran into one of your hoods already tonight."

He shook his head. "I sent no one to speak to you. What did this man look like? Tell me what he said." Varga looked almost afraid.

Sam described him. "He said he was from el Señor. He seems to think I have something he wants." She jerked against the hold but couldn't get enough leverage to free herself. "Let go of me."

"Not yet. I need to know more." He pushed her into one of the deck chairs. "This man is very dangerous. Do not speak to him again."

She relaxed. "You can let go of me. I'm not going to run away. I want answers as much as you do."

After a moment's consideration he released her, then took a seat opposite. "You would do well to obey el Señor. He does not like to lose what belongs to him." He fiddled with his knife, catching the light with his silver blade. If it was supposed to menace, it worked.

Sam changed her tone. "Look, I'd be happy to help if I had some idea what he was talking about, but I don't. Anyway, el Señor needn't be so cocky. I know he was at the mission compound that day, that he killed the padre. You were there, too. What were you looking for?"

"You really do not know?" He frowned when she shook her head. "Then why are you here?" He slid the blade against her cheek, under the loop of hair that caressed her cheek. "How did you know about the meeting?"

"I didn't. Someone sent me a note with a rose that said to be here at midnight to talk about the statue. I assumed it was Sanchez." She leaned forward. "How much do you want? Not that I'll give you anything until I see the statue."

"I do not have it."

"So you're here, why? Because you want to get it back?" She shook her head at his dejected look. "I don't know whether to be relieved it's out of your fumbling hands, or sorry that I'm going to have to keep tracking." She took a stab in the dark. "Did you ever have the real one?"

He shook his head. "Just a copy. To use as bait, so you would follow me." He glanced over his shoulder and surveyed the deck. His voice dropped. "I should not have told you that."

The whole thing was a scam! "But why? Who told you to do this?"

"El Zopilote." He shrugged. "I do not ask why."

"Who is he?"

"Nobody knows who el Zopilote is, *señorita*. But we know not to cross him."

"You were paid to fool me, but you never saw this guy's face?"

"Only a voice on *el teléfono* and *mucho dinero* for the trouble."

"Which you picked up at all those little stops along the way." Sam's heart sank at his nod. By now the trail was undoubtedly cold as ice. "So if you don't have it, who does?"

"Your *novio?*"

"My boyfriend—Daniel? I don't think so." She almost laughed. A shadow moved at the front of the deck. She lowered her voice. "Who is el Señor, Varga?"

"My boss." He shook his head rapidly. "I can say no more. Do not ask."

"But you said this el Zopilote paid you. Oh, never mind." He wasn't going to talk and she knew it. Sam thought for a moment. "Where's the real statue?"

"This I do not know."

"Can you find out? I'm not asking you to betray anyone. I didn't follow you so I could steal the statue. I've been authorized to buy it—if it's authentic. Can you find out if it is available?"

"And if it is?"

"Then I want an appraisal before I make an offer. My client will be generous." She thought quickly, trying to cover all the bases. "That's assuming you've cleared the way legally. The statue was left to a museum."

"It was stolen."

So he knew that. "By?"

"No more questions." He rose, rubbing the blade of his knife against his pants. "But I will tell you something. Be careful who you trust."

"That's cryptic." Sam thought quickly. "Are you including yourself?"

"I include everyone. Nothing is as it seems, *señorita.* There are men who care nothing for life. They have lost even their fear of God. Go home, where you came from."

"I can't do that, not without the statue. If you had it, would you trade it for the coins?"

A strange look covered his face, his whole body stance altered. He glanced around, then crouched in front of her, his voice a sibilant whisper. "You know of more coins?"

"Maybe. Why? Are you interested?"

A noise disrupted the silence around them. Varga's head jerked up as he scoured the area. "Be very quiet," he ordered. He looked panicked.

"Why?"

"Because playing games gets you killed. You saw that for yourself in the jungle."

"You're talking about el Padre Dulce?"

Varga said nothing, but his mouth pinched tight in a white line and he jerked his head in a nod.

The distinct shape of a human caught the moonlight for a second before a fleeting cloud obscured it. Different size, different shape. Sam assessed her situation, decided it was time to end this.

"My boss wants me to make a bid on that statue and that's what I'm going to do. Just find out who I talk to."

"I will try. Until then you must pretend to be only a tourist. Do not speak of the coins again, *señorita.* They will cause you much trouble."

He slipped away into the dark, leaving Samantha and the shadows alone on deck. Or almost. She turned her chair so her back was against the railing offering a clear view of the entire space.

"You can come out now," she murmured, raising her voice just a fraction above a whisper. "He's gone."

Obrigado stepped into the light. "You are most observant."

"Why Señor Obrigado, what a surprise to see you at last," she said, implying exactly the opposite. "Are you prepared to hear my bid on the statue?"

"Alas, the statue is not in my possession. But if you tell me your offer, I will pass it along to the one concerned."

"Why can't I do that?"

"I think that would not be wise, Ms. Henderson. But should you wish to discuss the matter of a chest of coins, I would be most happy to accommodate you in a trade."

"The coins for the statue, is that what you mean?"

He shrugged. "Perhaps."

"Why is it you think I have these coins in my possession?" she asked. "Because I have this one?" She flicked the gold disk attached to her wrist. "I assure you, I have only two."

"Because you gave the third to a bus driver." He spit out a Spanish epithet with dark menace. "Such stupidity."

"Sorry," she said, disgruntled by his tone. "I had no money and I needed to get out of that place. By the way, is the Peruvian minister of antiquities supposed to be trading stolen statues for coins?"

"My job is to preserve my country's history." He said it sanctimoniously, as if he were perfectly justified.

"Except that the statue isn't yours, and I'm not sure the coins are, either. Rumor has it they were found in international waters."

"Do not believe all you hear, *señorita.*" He lowered his voice as if he suspected someone was listening in. "Believe only what you see."

"Meaning?"

"I am a man who deals in the concrete, not the world of pretend." He buttoned his jacket, his eyes dark and unfathomable in the gloom, his voice sinister. "Talk to me when you have the coins. Then I can assure you I will be most ready to—how is the expression? Ah, yes. To talk the turkey."

Obrigado left. A moment later his footsteps clunked down the metal rungs and echoed into the night.

Sam remained on deck watching the horizon lighten as the rest of the clouds blew away. She tallied up what she knew. Varga hadn't expected her, Sanchez didn't show, but Obrigado wasn't surprised—because he'd sent the note. That had to mean he wanted those coins before someone else got them. It also meant he knew who had the statue.

In the midst of her thoughts a muffled scraping noise emanated from near the front of the deck. After checking to be sure she remained in the shadows, Sam waited, wondering who else would show up for this curious rendezvous. When no one appeared but the noises continued, she inched forward, striving for a better look. What she saw shocked her.

"Daniel!" When she hunched down, she saw his hands and feet were bound together. His lips were sealed with tape. "This is going to hurt." She ripped off the tape and slapped her hand over his mouth to smother his exclamation. "Sorry. What happened?"

"I got tied up," he muttered, as she untied his ropes. "Took you long enough."

"Sorry. I've been a little busy."

"I heard. Obviously Varga wanted me out of the way. He's the one who did this." Free of his fetters, he rose, took her arm and led her toward the stairs. "I need a cup of coffee. And some answers."

"Let's order it in the room," she murmured, shivering a little at the coolness she hadn't noticed before. Once they were safely inside their small space she placed the order while Daniel scrubbed the tape remains from his face. Sam sat down and began to list what she knew.

"What are you frowning about?" Daniel emerged from his room, accepted the tray when the steward arrived and tipped him. He poured out two rich black cups of coffee and handed her one, peering over her shoulder at the list.

"Sanchez and Varga are not working together."

"Because?" He sat down in the armchair, sipped his coffee, his eyes hidden.

"Varga never had the real statue, because he was working for this el Zopilote, making me feel like a sucker for following him. But he also works for el Señor and he's afraid of him, deathly afraid. What I don't know is which one he was working for when he was at the mission's compound. Obrigado's interest is obviously the coins." She tapped the pencil against her bottom lip, watched his reaction. "There's got to be a third party involved."

"My thoughts exactly."

Sam blinked. She was getting a funny feeling now and it had to do with the peculiar glint in his eyes. "Who's your suspect?"

"You won't like it." He took another drink as if to bolster his courage. "I have a lot of questions about Ric."

"Not this again!" Exasperated, she plunked down her pencil and leaned forward. "Obrigado's the one who said he could get the statue to trade. Ric doesn't go around stealing." Anger burst like fireworks inside her. She couldn't sit still. "You're letting your feelings impair your judgment, Daniel." She rose, ready to leave.

"My feelings aren't involved. Think about this rationally." His hand on her arm stopped her retreat. "Just consider the evidence, Samantha."

"You just said we have no proof." She sat down so she could be free of his touch. "Okay, explain."

Daniel pulled his chair nearer, so he was directly across from her. Then he began listing things, ticking each one off on his fingers.

"Ric knew you were tracking the statue."

"So did you, so did Varga."

His eyebrows rose. "Can I finish?"

"Go on."

"You saw him in Brazil and probably in Lima, too."

"How did you—" She clamped her lips shut, realizing she'd given herself away. "Go on."

"He showed up on the island—not just any island but one decidedly out of the main traffic flow, at a place most people wouldn't simply drop by, and he gave you some information."

"He said Varga was supposed to transport the statue to the Sanchez house, probably for his personal collection, but that it never got there."

"Which we know is a lie. Okay, I'll rephrase—incorrect." He inclined his head. "There's more."

"What else?" She was tired and fed up and ready to sleep for a very long time. But Samantha knew Daniel wouldn't stop yet.

"Why did we think Varga was working for Sanchez?" His eyes met hers. "Because Ric said so. But you never had anything to directly link the two men, did you?"

"Not really." She dragged her hair back, rubbed her neck. "Ric said he thought there might be someone with connections involved."

"Implying a government official—Obrigado? I can't help wondering why he said that. If he knew who it was, why didn't he tell?" Daniel tented his fingers under his chin. "You said a friend got his message to you. I'd be very interested in talking to his friend."

"So it's all a conspiracy? Boy, you really don't trust anyone, do you, Daniel?" She rose and walked toward her room, but just before she stepped inside, she turned. "Sometimes I feel sorry for you. You're always pushing someone away. Be careful, Daniel. Someday you'll push away the one who cares most about you. Then you'll be alone forever."

She left him sitting there and closed the door without making a sound.

Eventually Daniel turned out the lights in the cabin and went to sit on the balcony. The moon slid in and out of cloud cover, casting its glow on the waters slipping past.

Though Samantha might not know it, she was absolutely right. He didn't trust anyone. So many people had tailed him after his father's death, wanting handouts, freebies, donations. Uncle Bert had tried to shield him, but no matter where he went, someone had sought him out.

He'd thought Sam was different. But maybe she was at Finders to get information about his father—or rather his estate. Daniel concentrated on what he knew about her. She was the oldest child in a family of three children. Her father had died while she was in high school. Grant had found her through some contest he'd sponsored at a police academy and suggested she begin working for Finders as soon as her training was complete. As Grant had handled her background check, Daniel knew little more than her recent work history.

Time to change that. Daniel pulled out his phone and punched in an order for the Finders computer to download to him every last morsel of her history. What he read more than surprised him.

Sam wasn't just another pretty face. If she'd seemed cold toward him, she probably thought she had a right. Her father had been cleaned out by one of the infamous Howard McCullough stock deals. That action had plunged the family into bankruptcy after which Sam's father had taken his life.

He groaned. He could hardly bear to think that Sam was like all the rest—after the money. She'd seemed so genuine, so honest. But his father's greed and lust for more had damaged her family. It would be understandable if she wanted retribution. Pain arrowed straight to his heart and spread like a ripple in a pond. Not Sam, he begged silently. Please not Sam.

A beep from his telephone signaled more information. Sam had a sister in drug rehab and a younger brother who'd been involved in a series of petty crimes. According to the file, her mother had been under treatment for depression ever since her husband's death. Her whole family had been ruined by Howard McCullough. No wonder she had trust issues with him.

Daniel finished scouring the data, then closed the phone and set it on the table, wincing as his head continued its steady throbbing. He slid off his glasses and began to knead the bridge of his nose as he contemplated his next action. His gaze fell on the small Bible his uncle had given him, the Living Translation, Bert's favorite. Daniel leafed through absently, found himself in II Corinthians. Chapter 4.

> We are pressed on every side by troubles, but not crushed and broken. We are perplexed because we don't know why things happen as they do, but we don't give up. We are hunted down, but God never abandons us. We get knocked down, but we get up again and keep going.

Pressed on every side—that was him. Wary of Sanchez and Obrigado, distrustful of Ric, skeptical of Varga and now suspicious of his partner on this mission.

But the truth was staring him in the face. God never abandons. Okay then, Daniel wouldn't give up. He faced the hard truth; let it into the full light of day.

Sam didn't trust him. She thought he'd deliberately denied her a promotion because he was like his father. She'd lost her family to his father's greed and for that she resented him. But they had to get past that, needed to figure out what was going on with the statue. They had to finish the mission.

Or he could leave.

The idea tantalized him with its simplicity. Why not just walk away—tell Shelby the statue wasn't to be had and cancel the mission. Or hand it off to some other agency, someone not involved with Ric. Daniel was tempted to make this the first case Finders, Inc. had ever not solved, until an image of his uncle filled his mind. Bert had stuck by his decision to find those coins year after year. He'd triumphed because he hadn't given up. It was only proper that his uncle be listed as the discoverer. But that wouldn't happen unless they got those coins to the proper authorities.

Daniel sprawled in his chair, recalling the last time he'd spoken to his uncle.

Going diving and this time I'm going to bring them up. Our treasure is there, Danny boy. All we have to do is get it. Want to join me?

He hadn't gone because Shelby's daughter was missing and she'd needed him to keep Finders rolling. So once again he'd told Bert next time. Only next time hadn't come before Bert had died.

How the coins tied into the statue was a mystery, but that there was a connection was obvious. He closed his eyes to think about that for a moment. Sometime later Sam was shaking his shoulder.

"Daniel, wake up!"

He blinked and focused on her, aware that something was happening in the hallway. "What's wrong?" he asked.

"The fire alarm. We have to go to our station."

He took in her white terry robe and sandals and the way she avoided looking at him. In fact, she was almost to the door when he stopped her.

"Sam?"

"Yes?" She looked at him, her eyes wide with a hint of fear.

"Just in case it's a false alarm, what do we have that someone would want?" He pulled on his glasses as he spoke then pocketed his phone. Someone rapped on the door. He stepped into the main room and called, "We're coming," before he glanced around.

"I've got my coin," she murmured, "and my phone's in my pocket. "My purse is here. If you take your laptop I don't know what else there could be."

"Okay, let's go." He grabbed it and followed her out of the room and down the hall, trying to shelter her from the crush of frightened shipmates squeezing them into the tiny space. "Go in front of me," he urged, easing her ahead of him as they reached the stairs.

Sam would have turned off on the Sierra level, but Daniel urged her steadily upward to the top deck. She didn't argue, which probably meant she had as many questions as he did.

They worked their way to the front of the ship, huddling against the lookout cabin to stay out of the wind now fiercely blowing. Daniel tried to shield her as best he could while scanning the crowd.

"I don't recognize half of these people in their pj's," she joked as he helped her struggle into one of the life vests he'd brought with him.

Every cruise line feared fire at sea more than any other disaster and they took extreme precautions to make sure it didn't happen. Daniel didn't say it as he fastened the clasps on her vest, then secured his own, but he kept searching for some wisp of smoke in the predawn light. He winced when Sam's fingernails dug into the skin of his forearm.

"Daniel, look!"

He scanned the deck. "I don't see—"

"By the stairs," she whispered.

He caught his breath as two of the crew carried someone up the stairwell and laid the body on the deck, then placed a blanket over top.

"Isn't that the same stairs we went down when we got locked in?" Her voice barely reached him.

Daniel nodded but said nothing. Instead he searched the faces of his shipmates.

An announcement declared the fire alarm a mistake and assured the passengers that the ship was perfectly safe, that they were in no danger. The message was repeated in Spanish, French and German. Passengers were urged to return to their rooms or, if they still felt uncomfortable, to go to the main dining room where hot chocolate and tea would be served as well as a complimentary drink for those whose nerves were affected.

"We're not going anywhere, Samantha," he told her. "Play along with me." He drew her near the rail and wrapped his arm around her waist as they stared out at the sea.

"You folks all right?" The purser stood behind them, his face drawn tight.

"We're fine. Sam's just a little queasy so we thought we'd stay here till her stomach settled, get a bit of air." Daniel strove for a troubled note. "She and a friend had an argument and she hasn't seen him in a couple of days. I don't suppose that could be him over there?" He tilted his head toward the body.

"Don't think so. It looks like it's one of the crew, though we haven't identified him yet."

Sam faked a gasp. Daniel patted her hand, told her to stay there, and then drew the purser away. "Her friend was one of the crew," he murmured. "Are you sure she couldn't take a look, just to ease her mind?" He added more persuasion when the man seemed to hesitate. "She's really had a tough time on this ship, getting drugged and that food poisoning and all."

The man's face altered. "I suppose it will be all right, though they'll be moving the body as soon as the doctor arrives."

"Thanks." Daniel shepherded Sam toward the blanket-covered form. "Take it easy now, darling." The purser offered a sympathetic smile then slowly peeled back the blanket, revealing the face.

Sam's gasp was so real even Daniel was fooled. She covered her mouth with her hand, turned her face into his shoulder. "It's Varga," she told him, her voice cracking.

"It's not her friend. Thank you." Daniel wrapped his arm around her waist. "Poor fellow, he looks so peaceful. What did he die of?"

"Smoke inhalation, we think. Someone blocked one of the vents into a mechanical room. Somehow the door was locked."

"Well, thank you for doing this." Since Samantha was trembling, he led her to the ship's railing to calm down. "He'll turn up, just have faith, dear. Deep breaths now." They stood together until the body was gone and the staff had left.

To the east streaks of orange-pink striated the blue sky, bathing the world in the soft halo of sunrise.

"Are you all right?" he whispered when she finally drew away from him.

"Yes. Thank you." She looked like a little girl awakening from a nightmare, the stains of tears still bathing her cheeks. "Someone killed him, Daniel. We both know that."

He nodded.

"Maybe it's my fault because he said too much last night." Her eyes spilled tears. "Or maybe someone didn't like the idea of him helping me. But to kill him…"

"You can't blame yourself, Samantha. You didn't do it." He pointed. "Look. Clear sky."

As if they'd floated from one weather system to another, the colors disappeared and the sun stretched a tentative finger over the horizon. In the distance an island appeared across an expanse of smooth water.

"Amazing, isn't it?" he whispered, awed by the power so quickly leashed. "Reminds me of Moses crossing the Red Sea. One minute there was no path, the next it was dry."

She angled her head like a curious bird, her expression puzzled. "You really take all that stuff literally, don't you?"

"If by stuff you mean the Bible, then—" he nodded "—yes. I believe in a God who created all this. I can't imagine it would be impossible for Him to push the water back with one puff of His breath. His might, His strength, His gentleness—it's all part of His person. Sometimes I think I know Him and then I realize that I've only begun to scratch the surface of who God is."

"I used to believe in Him," she murmured, so softly he wondered if she'd wanted him to hear. "A long time ago."

"Before my father ruined yours?" he asked.

She stilled. "How did you know about that?"

"It's true, isn't it?" He waited until she finally nodded. "I'm sorry he did that, Samantha. So sorry."

"Somehow, it doesn't seem to matter so much this morning." She stared across the water, her voice contemplative. "My father had such big plans for his investment. I was going to college, my sister was going to live in Paris and finish the art course she'd started. My brother was going to get his dream of owning his own car-repair business. It was all arranged."

"And my father stole that from you." He laid a hand on hers. "If I could bring your father back, Sam, I would. But I can't. I can't fix what he did. I can only say I'm sorry."

"I know." She looked over her shoulder at the spot where Varga had lain. "It's the waste of a life that gets to me. My father didn't value his life, his wife, and his children enough to live for them." The words whispered out on a sigh. "Greed killed all our dreams. What a waste."

As he watched her, Daniel realized how big the chasm between them was. No matter what, she'd always see his father in him.

Suddenly her body language altered, her whole form seemed to tense, grow rigid. "Listen." The ship was moving very slowly now, yet a noise, the sound of another motor, penetrated.

As quietly as he could, Daniel crossed the deck and looked down. A small boat steered away from them toward the island. There was only one man on board, but his back was to them.

"Someone's coming, Daniel. Quickly." Sam drew him into the shadows behind a large Ping-Pong table secured to the railing. Two men appeared. They moved to the same place Daniel and Sam had been standing a few minutes before, watched the boat.

"He's gone," Obrigado said in Spanish.

"For now. But he will be back," Sanchez replied. "He does not yet have what he seeks. Until he does, we could all meet Varga's fate."

"I do not think el Señor killed Varga."

"Then who—"

"Varga spoke to the girl of The Vulture. He should not have said it. We must stay out of it, Eduardo. Your business is the statue. Mine is to find those coins. As for the rest…" Obrigado shrugged. "El Señor does not need our help."

"Tomorrow is the auction. I was assured I would have the statue by now." Sanchez smacked the railing with his palm. "Where is it?"

"The woman?"

"I am beginning to believe that was a lie. She knows nothing."

"That can't be. I was assured she would lead us to the coins. We must think of a plan. Otherwise…" Obrigado did not finish the statement.

Several moments later the two left the deck and clambered down the stairs. When he was certain they were alone, Daniel slipped free from his hiding place to scan the water. He could see no sign of the small boat bobbing on the water. Whoever it was had apparently disappeared.

"You don't believe that boat was carrying Varga's body away?" Sam studied his face. "So who was on it?"

"El Señor?" He grasped her elbow. "Come on, we might as well go back to the cabin. People will soon be stirring."

"Yes." She walked across the deck. "If el Señor didn't kill Varga, then who did?"

"Good question."

He followed her down the stairs to their room. "Try to get a bit of a rest, Sam. Maybe it will look clearer in the morning." He watched the door close behind her before he returned to his place on the balcony and pulled out his phone.

"Sorry to wake you, Shelby, but I think I've just remembered why I recognized Ric Preston. I need you to look up newspaper articles. Maybe, just maybe we've finally got something to go on."

TEN

"Two days before we return to port." Sam looked sideways at Daniel. "And I'm still in the dark about the statue."

He speared another slice of grapefruit but didn't comment. Sam gave up trying to coax a response out of him.

"I've been so busy fussing and fuming over this case, I've barely seen half of what was offered," she told him half-defiantly. "Today there's a tour to see the giant tortoises that the Galapagos Islands are named for. The concierge really pushed it. I think I'll go, take some pictures. At least I won't go home totally empty-handed and it will be a chancc to get off this boat for a few hours."

Daniel still said nothing and remained silent until they had landed on the island.

"Is there somewhere specific you want to go?" she asked, trying to fathom why he was so quiet.

"I'm not leaving you alone. I'll go wherever you want." He held up his hand to stop her protest. "Let's not waste time arguing. I'm not going to change my mind."

She decided not to argue. "There's a bus to see the twin pit craters they talked about. Los Gemelos. The

Twins." She peered down at the folder. The departure point was circled in red. "I hope he gets a commission."

"Over there." He pointed, then followed her to the bus.

The seats were narrow. Daniel seemed very close. Sam could even smell his cologne. She tried to ignore that and his silence as the guide explained what their agenda entailed.

"This morning you will experience seven different vegetation zones," he explained. "That's just another detail that makes Santa Cruz Island and the Galapagos so special. Before we reach the craters, however, we will be stopping at a tortoise reserve where you may view the animals in their natural habitat. Please sit back and enjoy our tour."

The bus was about to pull away when two men rapped on the door and climbed up the steps. Though they were dressed in uniforms bearing the Charles Darwin Research Center logo, both the bus driver and the tour guide seemed puzzled by their sudden appearance.

All the seats were full, leaving them nowhere to sit, a fact which the bus driver and the guide took some pains to point out. The driver was particularly disgruntled and pointed repeatedly to the sign which said all passengers must remain seated while the bus was in motion. Some hissed whispering took place and finally the two were allowed to remain on the bus if they stood at the back. As they walked past Sam one man bumped Daniel's shoulder. In the apology that ensued a small bit of paper fluttered to the floor at her feet. Then both moved to the back of the bus and remained standing there.

The seats were close together and Sam had to wiggle around to retrieve the paper.

"What are you doing?"

She snatched it up and straightened, then opened her palm so he could see what was inside. After unfolding it, she read the words silently.

Lonesome George. Wait.

Puzzled, she looked at Daniel. "What does that mean?"

He shrugged. "No clue."

As their guide began describing the terrain, Sam tucked the paper into her pocket. Maybe the concierge's insistence she come here wasn't coincidental. Someone had taken the trouble to get her this message so she might as well play along for now.

Daniel followed her around the twin pit craters, barely commenting on the highland terrain or the elusive vermilion flycatchers their guide pointed out. Sam tried to drum up conversation while they ate lunch at a place simply called "the Ranch," but found little success since Daniel was immersed in his own thoughts. She heaved a sigh of relief when they walked back outside into the hot sun. Ten long minutes later they reboarded the bus.

"Now, my friends, we have a great treat in store for you," the tour guide announced, clasping his hands together as if he could hardly wait. "We are on our way to visit a tortoise reserve. Here you will be able to admire the giant tortoises and their one-year-old offspring, which are part of the breeding program here on the island."

Daniel visibly perked up at this announcement, though he continued to scan faces aboard the bus. "Our friends did not get back on."

Sam spotted them standing near the rear of the Ranch, watching as the bus rumbled away. Neither one seemed worried.

"Apparently they only wanted on to contact you. Any ideas about 'George'?"

Sam shook her head. At the tortoise reserve she spent a lot of time searching for the two men or anyone else who didn't seem to belong. To no avail. Everyone was totally captivated by the antics of the small tortoises, especially Daniel.

"It's really unbelievable how this species has survived all these years."

After a while, she got tired of just standing there and wandered to a summit where she could look down at the prickly pear cactus forest and the many land birds that fluttered above it.

"I'm going to come back sometime," Daniel murmured from just behind her. "I feel I've only seen about a quarter of what this place has to offer. My father always talked about visiting Galapagos but somehow the treasure he was after always seemed to come first."

Daniel always said "my father." Not Dad or Pops, or any of the other more familiar terms children use. Perhaps this was his way of distancing himself from the man who'd hurt him with his coldness.

"I see all this and I feel insignificant in God's grand scheme of things." He pointed at the birds. "They've adapted and changed to their environment's needs, changing weather patterns, pollution and people. Makes me feel foolish for clinging to my set ways, thinking I can predict what will happen in the future. I never predicted I'd be alone, without Bert."

The sadness in his voice touched some place deep inside and Sam couldn't stop herself from reaching out and touching his arm. "You're not alone, Daniel."

"Aren't I?" He glanced down at her, his eyes inscrutable behind the dark lenses.

"No, of course not. You have friends—Shelby and Tim care a great deal about you."

"As I care about them."

"I'm sure you have lots of other friends, too."

"Debatable. I haven't had time to keep up with them, haven't made it a priority, I should say. I've been too busy worrying about Finders. Buried myself in my work." A dry note entered his voice as his lips tipped in a half smile. "You were partially right, you know. I've become a workaholic, just like my father."

"I don't think you're like him at all. I should never have said what I did."

"You were right even if you didn't know him." He stared forward, apparently enthralled by what he saw.

"I know you. In a way that gives me an insight into him. He didn't know how to be a father. I think your uncle knew that and tried to fill in for him."

"Uncle Bert was good at giving. I'm going to miss him." He tilted his head down, kicked at a stone on the ground. "I got a message on my cell. The mission society is holding a funeral for him in two days."

"We'll be back from this cruise in time for it then." Pained that he hadn't told her earlier, Sam told herself she deserved it.

He turned as a holler from the bus alerted them to its departure. "We'd better go."

"Okay." She walked beside him, her mind trying to figure out why he'd told her. "Can I go with you, Daniel? To the funeral, I mean?"

"Why?" He stopped, pulled off his glasses and frowned at her. "You didn't know him."

"Yes, I did," she whispered, remembering. "He saved my life. I'd like a chance to say goodbye."

He studied her for a long time before nodding. "If you want."

The bus rumbled back over the track and finally stopped next to the research station. Their guide had a few last words.

"Please feel free to check out the museum collection, the herbarium, the nursery and native gardens," he urged. "Marine vessels used all around the islands are located to the left. The station houses dining facilities and the Van Straelen Visitors Center where you can learn more about the conservation work being done here in Galapagos. They also offer explanations about how you can support us. Thank you for coming. Enjoy."

Everyone clapped then began gathering their things preparatory to leaving. Suddenly the guide's voice burst through the chatter.

"I have forgotten one important thing," he explained. "You must be sure to see Lonesome George, the last surviving tortoise of the subspecies from Pinta Island. He is a most important member of Santa Cruz."

Sam looked at Daniel. "Lonesome George," she whispered excitedly. "He's a tortoise."

"I heard." Daniel glanced around. "Over there."

They climbed off the bus and headed for the pen where Lonesome George seemed perfectly happy sunning himself despite the curious stares showered on him.

"How long do you think we'll have to wait for whoever sent that note to make contact?" She checked around, searching for some familiar face that would explain the mystery.

"No idea." He took his stance at the side of the pen and stared at the huge tortoise. "Think how long this animal has lived, how many things it has weathered. Compared to George here, I've barely touched my toes in the water of life. But I'll bet he's done way less whining."

"Huh?" Sam was surprised and a little confused by his words.

"Look at him. The man said he'd come here from another island. That means old George was uprooted, moved out of the familiar and stuck in a place where he has no family, no friends and probably nothing that was familiar. George isn't complaining about it, though. He's decided to make the best of it, catch some rays and wait to see what pops up for dinner."

Sam giggled. "He's a tortoise, Daniel. He doesn't get much choice."

"Sure he does. He could handle this situation in any number of ways. But he chooses to make the best of it." Daniel surveyed the pen, took stock of what was there. "He probably grew up waddling in and out of the ocean whenever he felt like it. Now he's got a pretend pond that's not nearly as big as the ocean. On the upside, somebody feeds him regularly and if he gets too hot, he doesn't have to hunt for shade, it's already been thought of. Makes me ashamed of how I handle changes in my own life."

"You want to be in a pen and have somebody look after you?" she asked, raising one eyebrow.

"Maybe not quite yet, thanks." He grinned. "I'm just saying that there is more than one way to handle things and lately I'd forgotten that."

"You don't like your life?"

Daniel shrugged. "I was getting a little bored. Probably boring, too. I enjoyed fieldwork. Leaving it was hard. Lately I've been dwelling on the negative—never getting out of the office, never free from the telephone. Coming here was a wake-up call and God knew I needed that."

"You think God brought us here?" She struggled to wrap her mind around the concept. "I thought we came after a statue. Or at least I did. I guess you came after me."

"Believe me, God worked all that together to bring us here."

"Here—to Lonesome George. Why?"

"So we could get more answers."

"We hope." She thought about it a moment, then spoke, hesitantly lest he take offense. "Either way, I don't think God should get much credit in this circumstance. It just happened."

"Not to me. I believe God has a hand in everything that happens in my life, including coming here."

She considered it. "Maybe you," she conceded. "But God doesn't have anything to do with me."

"Of course He does. He has everything to do with you." He motioned to a nearby bench, walked beside her to it. "God is the reason you're here, Samantha. He created you. He loves you and wants to have a relationship with you."

She almost laughed at the thought. "Why me?"

"Because you're His child and He loves you. Those who know Him find Him infinitely loving. He's always there, always listening, always willing to lead and direct. All He asks is that we trust Him to do what is best for us."

She struggled with the concept for a while and found herself snagged on that word again—trust.

"I don't know about your God, but my guess is He's probably waiting for me to mess up so He can have a good laugh." She could tell he didn't like that.

"God would never laugh at you, Sam. God is love."

"So you say." She'd argued this in her own mind a hundred times. "So that great love—that's what got my mother so depressed that she barely even knows me anymore? Is your great God's love why my sister can only go about an hour without a case of the shakes from needing the next fix? Is that why my brother can't see any hope in his future, because God loves Him so much?

"I don't know." He didn't look away from her glare, though his lips tightened. "I'm sure their problems have more to do with my father and his actions, but that doesn't mean God abandoned you or your family. Maybe you need to ask Him for help."

"Because God is going to send me some thunderbolt answers to my family's problems?"

He half smiled at her angry tone. "I don't know what God will do. And neither do you until you ask Him. What I do know is that He is able to do above and beyond all that we can ask or think."

"That sounds like something your uncle would say."

"Maybe because he knew it was true." Daniel leaned back against the bench and sighed, eyes inscrutable behind the dark lenses. "Uncle Bert was at a place in his life where he didn't seem to need to ask God many questions anymore. He had lots of problems, but he always seemed confident that if he asked God's direction, an answer would be given to him. He had learned to trust. Sometimes I envied him that confidence."

"So do I." She chewed her bottom lip, wondering if she dared say it. "I agonize over every decision I make. It's hard to know how to help Mom, what treatment will be best, whether or not the place she's in will take good care of her."

"Sounds difficult." He reached down and grasped her fingers with his, squeezed them. "If I can do anything, I'd like to. After all, it was my father that ruined their lives."

"We don't need charity, Daniel."

"I wasn't offering charity. I was offering friendship. And help. If you need it." He dragged off his sunglasses and rubbed his temple. "Isn't that why you came to Finders, Inc. and looked up information on my father—to find out whether or not his estate could cover some of the expense? Well, it can. Easily."

"I don't—"

"Don't what? Want my money? You'd be the first." He rose and stalked over to the pen, his body language impossible to ignore.

Daniel was furious. And hurt. He didn't deserve to be. Daniel might not know it but he was exactly like his uncle, always reaching out to someone in need of help. Last month Joel in security had told her how Daniel had helped him organize a search for his adopted daughter's birth mother by explaining how to set up a Web page and use the Internet to find leads. Not charity, generosity.

She walked to the pen. "I was rude. Thank you for offering."

He turned, his face tight, eyes narrow. "Why do you always think the worst of me, Samantha? It wasn't I who stole your money, it was my father. And I assure you I am nothing like him."

"I know that." Sam sighed. "I know you're honest and upright, that you have integrity that wouldn't allow you to do what he did."

"Do you really know it? Or are you just saying what you think I want to hear?" He reached out and clasped her shoulder. "There's someone coming."

Sam saw a man in a white shirt and dark pants walking toward them. He held a small package in one hand. "Do you know who he is?"

Daniel shook his head.

"You are Ms. Henderson?" The man waited politely for her response and, when she nodded, held out the package. "This is for you."

"Oh." She accepted it from him, staring at her name scrawled across it.

"Where did you get this from?" Daniel asked.

"Dr. Beselli asked me to deliver it."

"Dr. Beselli?" She glanced at Daniel to see if the name rang any bells. Apparently not.

"He is working on some research here at the station. I am his assistant."

"May we speak with Dr. Beselli? It's very important. I'm sorry I don't know your name." Daniel had placed himself so the man would have to move around him to return to the station.

"I am Alexander. Dr. Beselli is very busy but sometimes he talks to tourists, answers questions. Please follow me." The man stopped before the main entrance and led them inside. "Dr. Beselli, I am very sorry to disturb you but these people wish to speak with you." Alexander waited, hands folded, for the man in the white lab coat to turn away from his test tubes.

"What people are these, Alexander?" He frowned fiercely, his blue eyes angry. "I cannot chat with the tourists. I have work to do."

"We won't bother you for long, sir. We just want to ask you about this package Alexander delivered to Ms. Henderson. Do you happen to know where it came from?"

The doctor stepped forward to get a closer look at what lay in Sam's hands. "Oh, yes. That package. A man asked me to give it to the lady. I didn't know him, but he seemed very intent on her receiving it and I wanted him to leave so I agreed."

"When was this?" Sam wondered if Ric had been on this island, as well.

"This morning. A boatload of those blasted tourists were poking around and I suppose he was one of them, because he said he couldn't do it himself or he'd miss his ship. The *Magdalena* I think, or maybe the *Magellan,* was it, Alexander?"

But Alexander had left.

"That man disappears at the drop of a hat." Dr. Beselli glared at the door as if to will him back. "Now what was I saying? Oh, yes, the package. I have no idea what's in it, I'm afraid. No idea at all. Anything else?"

"Could you describe the man?" Sam asked in a last-ditch hope.

"Hmm. I'm afraid I never pay much attention to these things. Let's see. He was tall. Taller than you, young man. And dark skinned. Latin American, I should think. A slight accent—English. He wore a white shirt and black pants with white shoes. Didn't suit at all, those shoes. Not the kind for a tourist on this island, no sir. Should have left them on his boat." He turned away to accept the steaming mug of something Alexander brought him. "I think we shall repeat that last experiment, Alex. I'm not entirely certain our results are accurate."

They'd learned everything they were going to. Sam lifted a hand to wave. "Thank you. We appreciate the help. I hope your experiment is a success."

"A success, she says. As if these things are ever a success. Rules out another possibility, that's all. Just another possibility."

"I will lock the door behind you." Alexander ushered them out.

"Thank you." As Sam preceded Daniel out the door, she found herself being propelled forward. "What are you doing?"

"Don't open that yet. We've got five minutes left to catch the last tender that will take us back to the ship. Someone was cutting it pretty fine."

By the time they got in line, Sam was parched. "I want one of those bottles of soda."

He bought her drink, a bottle of water and a peach from a little wagon. Sam rinsed off the peach with some of his water. Once they were seated in the launch she tasted it, let the smooth, cool tingle of the pineapple drink slide down her throat. "Much better."

Daniel said nothing, but his eyes were constantly roving back and forth.

"What do you think is in it?" she asked, staring at the packet in her lap.

"We'll open it in the room. If it passes security."

"Oh." She stared at him. "I never thought of that."

He continued his scrutiny of the other ships in harbor.

"There's no *Magdalena* or *Magellan,* I checked. You won't find him here."

"Maybe not." But that didn't stop him from looking.

She'd been thinking about his earlier comments. Here in public it seemed like a good time to broach the subject again. "Can I ask a favor?"

"Of me?" He took off his sunglasses as if suspicious. "I guess."

"I was just wondering if you had any connections that you could ask about care homes in the city. In Victoria, I mean. Mom's place is okay for the moment. But it would be nice if her treatment was a little more specific to her individual case. She only goes to group sessions now."

He sat there staring at her, as if she'd turned green and grown two noses. Sam flushed. "I'm sorry. I shouldn't have asked. Never mind."

He shook his head, a slight smile twisting his lips. "You can't take it back, Samantha. You asked for my help. Did you mean it?"

She nodded, trying to fathom what lay behind the strange note in his voice. "Yes. Thank you."

"Don't thank me yet. I haven't done anything. But I will send out a few feelers. Where is she now?"

Sam told him, offered a few other particulars. By the time they'd reached the ship she was embarrassed by her own temerity in asking the head of Finders, Inc. to help her mother.

"Give me the parcel while you climb up," he ordered, but there was a note in his voice she hadn't heard before, a sort of suppressed excitement that made her wonder about its cause.

The package passed security with no problem. Back in their room, she ripped open the paper. A picture fell out.

"The statue. So it finally appears." He bent over to pick it up, but Sam beat him to it, her fingers brushing his as she snatched up the snapshot.

"Look at this," she exclaimed.

He leaned over her shoulder, scanned the scribbled words. "Be at the Inca Museum, Lima, in two days at 7:30 p.m. if you want it." His eyes narrowed. "Meaning it won't be at the auction tonight."

"I guess not. Do you think Sanchez sent this?" She twisted her head to stare at him.

"Drawing us to his own museum? Not likely."

"So who's leading us to the statue?"
He stared at the picture for a very long time.
"Maybe someone who's coaxing us into a trap."

ELEVEN

"Going once, twice, three times—sold for twenty-five thousand American dollars. And that, ladies and gentlemen, is the end of our Inca gold auction. We hope your trinkets from our treasure chest will give you joy and—"

"Let's get out of here." Daniel tucked his hand under Sam's arm and escorted her from the huge salon and the crush of people gathered there.

"The whole evening—a waste." He'd hoped, prayed, an answer would be in the auction.

"I want to go to the reception, Daniel." Sam looped her arm through his, her smile the same adoring pretense she'd worn all evening. He didn't like it any better now.

"I don't—"

"I saw Obrigado go in there," she explained. "I want to talk to him. Have some faith in me, will you?"

How did you deny anything to a woman who looked like she'd stepped off a cloud? He followed her willingly, obediently sampled the chocolate fountain as soft music filled in the gaps of conversation. He'd just decided to sip a cup of coffee when Sam gave a warning tug on his sleeve.

"Señor Sanchez, it's so lovely to see you. And Señor

Obrigado. Are you here to make sure no Peruvian artifacts were smuggled aboard?" She smiled sweetly at both men.

Daniel stood back and watched her work, marveling at the grace and iron will she concealed in a gossamer white satin sheath. Neither man was averse to ogling her, but he was certain both knew exactly what she was talking about.

"Do you have some Peruvian artifacts you are trying to smuggle?" Obrigado asked, one eyebrow quirked upward.

"The only jewelry I have is my little coin. Oh, and the earrings Daniel bought me, of course." She tilted her head to show them the gold studs, then held out her wrist. "Señor Sanchez can tell you I didn't steal this. A friend gave it to me."

"A close friend?"

"Daniel's uncle, actually." She turned toward Sanchez. "Daniel told me he was discussing my statue with you."

The curator frowned at Daniel. "You have acquired it?"

"Not yet. Sam's a little overeager. I did get a photo if you'd like to see it." He pulled the one they'd received from his pocket and carefully unfolded it. "You can see that someone told us to go to your museum. I thought, hoped, that meant you'd found it."

"I—I—" Sanchez paled, turned to Obrigado. "I don't know what this means."

"You must have heard about it, Señor Obrigado. It was to be given to a museum, in Rio I think it was. Anyway it was stolen. I tracked it all the way down here, but now I've lost it. And I really *really* want that statue for my collection." Her appeal sounded heartrending as she glanced from one man to the other.

"*Señorita,* I do not wish—"

"Well, if you can't help, you can't. I guess we'll just have to go to this Inca Museum and see the person who sent this note." She turned away, gasped and turned back. "Neither one of you sent me this picture, did you?"

The both shook their heads.

"It was worth a try. Come on, honey. I want some more of that chocolate." She tucked her arm in Daniel's, fluttered the arm with the bracelet.

"Excuse me, *señorita.* May I take a closer look at the coin?" Obrigado had it in his fist before she could object and began to study it.

"Certainly. I did have three you know. Daniel has one, too. We love them. Goodness knows how many more are floating about, though. There could be a whole chest full of them somewhere. A treasure chest." She laughed, tugged her arm free. "Goodbye, gentlemen. Or perhaps, *adios.*" She gave a quick, trembly laugh then drew Daniel toward the fountain. "I sure hope they have strawberries. I adore strawberries."

He played along, dipping tiny wild strawberries into the chocolate and feeding them to her, longing to kiss her chocolate lips. When they finally left the room, Daniel noticed the two men, heads bent together, whispering in a corner. Once they were safely inside their room, he studied her. "What was that about?"

"I thought it was time to throw a little grease on the fire," she told him, grinning. "All we have to do now is get to the Inca Museum. Those two will be there and I wouldn't be surprised if the statue showed up, too."

Daniel wished he felt as confident.

As the shoreline drew nearer Daniel wondered at his mixed feelings. It would be a relief to get off the ship and away from this beautiful, mesmerizing, infuriating woman. A relief and a wrench, because now he was more certain than ever that Samantha was the only woman who could fill the hole in his heart.

This morning she had awakened him at the crack of dawn with a thump on his door, insisting he go with her topside to watch their arrival into San Cristóbal. He'd come along, not through a sense of duty, but because their time together would soon be over.

Today she wore a white dress with slashes of dark green surging up from the hem, and the infamous white sandals. Her glossy curls danced in the breeze as she leaned over the railing, trying to see more. Though her fake tan had lightened, her skin still retained a dark honey tone. The past two hours of direct sunshine had left a dusky flush on her cheekbones that reminded him of those juicy peaches she loved so much. Samantha Henderson was tantalizing.

"I enjoyed this cruise, Daniel." Her green eyes looked huge below that black cap of hair. Cutting it had only made her seem more vulnerable.

"So did I." He sought for the right words, and then decided to just tell her. "The mission society sent the location of the funeral. You don't have to go."

"I want to."

"It's not necessary. I don't expect it and Uncle Bert certainly wouldn't."

"I'm not going because someone expects me to. I'm going because he was a kind man who helped me when I needed it and I want to say goodbye to him. If you don't want me to go, just say so." Her eyes snapped with temper.

"It's not that. I thought it might be better if you stayed

at a hotel, waited in safety. We still don't know who we're dealing with." The truth was he wanted her there, beside him, as he said farewell to the man who'd been more of a father than his own.

"I'm going."

"Good." That took her by surprise. After a moment of intense scrutiny she turned to watch the dolphins. Daniel grinned. "No argument, Samantha?"

She glanced over one shoulder, her saucy eyes dancing. "Why argue? I got what I wanted." After a moment she spoke again, but this time her voice had changed. "I'm sure you'll miss him. If you want to talk about him sometime, remember him, I'll be happy to listen."

"Thanks." Sometime when? When she left Finders?

"Daniel, I was thinking about what you said—about God." She turned her face into the breeze, closing her eyes. "I kept praying and praying—and nothing happened. Nothing good anyway."

He touched her shoulder, waited for her to turn. "That's when you have to pray harder, Samantha. That's when the doubts and fears are standing there, ready to climb all over you. That's when you have to know that God is right beside you, that you're going to come shining through. I found this verse the other day." He pulled out his tiny Bible, flipped it open and read.

> "We are pressed on every side by troubles, but not crushed and broken. We are perplexed because we don't know why things happen as they do, but we don't give up."

She took over.

"We are hunted down, but God never abandons us. We get knocked down, but we get up again and keep going."

"It's a promise," he told her.

She said nothing, simply stared at the words. Finally she turned back to the water. The harbor grew closer. He felt a twinge of regret knowing the fragile bond they'd shared would soon be over, changed by the world they were returning to.

"What shall we do first?" she asked.

"Get back to Lima. Find a hotel. Change. Then I want to get some flowers. The service will begin at two. That won't allow for much dawdling. At least I managed to get through to Shelby. Our flights to Lima are booked."

She seemed content to let him take control as they finally stepped off the ferry and disembarked to pick up their bags dockside.

Daniel grabbed them and urged her toward the waiting line of cabs. They made it to the airport in record time and boarded their plane without mishap. Once they'd deplaned in Lima, he gave the name of a hotel Shelby had booked to the driver, then sat back, content to watch the city fly past.

The hotel was new, elegant and had appointed them to a suite with adjoining rooms, much larger than they'd had on the ship.

"Is half an hour long enough for you?" he asked after he'd dumped her case, the one the cruise ship had replaced, on the bed.

"Yes."

He left her to it, took his bag to his own room and

stripped before stepping under the shower. The water poured over him in a strong, steady pulse. *We are hunted down, but God never abandons us.* He let that sink in until a tapping at his door disturbed him.

"Daniel? A man is here with flowers. Do you want to look at them first or should I choose some?"

"Just a minute." He toweled off, pulled on his clothes then walked into the sitting area. He knew exactly what he wanted, what Uncle Bert would have loved. "White orchids," he told the man in Spanish. "Lots of white orchids, with red stripes if you have them. He said they reminded him of peppermints."

The florist seemed to understand. He chose a huge number, arranged them into a design and passed them over. He accepted his money, turned to go. At the door he paused. "Permit me to offer a warning, *señor.* El Padre Dulce was well loved in this country. He did much to help those who could not help themselves. There are many who are angry his killer has not been found. It would be best to expect a crowd at the church."

"Thank you. We will be prepared." Daniel showed the man the door after slipping him a tip.

"How did he know where we were going?" Sam asked once the door was closed.

"My name, I suspect. Bert's was the same."

"Yes, of course." She wore a navy skirt, white shirt and sandals. Her straw bag swung over one shoulder. "Are you ready to leave?"

"Just a moment more." It was probably too hot for a jacket but Daniel pulled one on anyway. It helped conceal the gun the florist had slipped into his palm. There could be more than grateful parishioners to worry about. Shelby had thought of everything. When he was ready he opened the door.

"I haven't seen you wear that before," he said, noting the way the clothes hugged her curves.

"I asked someone in the boutique downstairs to send up something suitable for a funeral. This is what they chose." She twirled around for him.

"You look lovely, Samantha."

"You always do that," she murmured as she walked out the door in front of him.

"Do what?" he asked, wondering how he'd offended her this time.

"You call me Samantha when you offer a compliment or get serious."

"Oh." How often had he given himself away to her, exposed his feelings? "I'll be more careful."

She stopped in the hall. "I wasn't criticizing you, Daniel. I was just commenting."

He didn't know how to respond to that so Daniel kept his own counsel. By the time they arrived at the church, his nerves were so tight the screech of brakes in the next street had him gripping the car door. Sam glanced at his clenched hand but said nothing. As they trod up the staircase she slipped her fingers under his arm as if to offer some kind of moral support. He wanted to tell her he didn't need it, but that would have been a lie. He needed her there, with him, to help him say goodbye to the man he'd loved more than his own father.

The church was a massive structure built in Spanish colonial times. But Daniel found his attention drawn to the front. At first he couldn't look away from the flower-draped coffin that rested there, couldn't force himself to believe that Bert was inside, that he would never burst out laughing or slap him on the back again. But then he saw beyond the coffin, to the altar and the scene of Christ standing above Mary in Gethsemane.

That was his Lord. It dawned on him then that this same Christ had also been the source of his uncle's faith. It might take years to stop thinking that he'd have to ask Bert about this or tell Bert that, but Bert had been reunited with God in an instant. This was not a time to mourn.

The service passed like a mirage as men Bert had worked with spoke of his life, his dedication, his love for Peru and its people. When it came time for his eulogy, Daniel set his orchids on the floor in front of the coffin. The top already overflowed. Then he moved behind the pulpit.

He looked at the faces, found Sam's, saw her tiny smile of encouragement and took a deep breath.

"Father Bert was my uncle," he told them simply. "My uncle, my friend, my pastor, my father, my teacher—and so much more. But Bert was first and foremost God's child. What he wanted to do most was to serve his Lord, and for Bert the best place to do that was the jungle. He loved it there. Whenever he'd visit me he could hardly wait to return."

The host of eyes stayed on him.

"Uncle Bert is finished his work here now. He's done all he can. But the job isn't finished. The people he loved still need someone to teach them about God. We don't yet know who that will be or if they'll be allowed the same freedoms he was. But we know the void will be filled. God's work will go on."

He paused, waited for the soft press of assurance and knew he had to say it.

"If my uncle Bert helped you in any way, if he taught you something, if he loved you when you needed it most, if he touched your life in a way that made it better, would you honor his memory by passing that on? Bert couldn't get to everyone. But you and I can. Together."

In the silence of the great church, Daniel returned to his seat. Several moments later the leader of his uncle's mission rose, offered a prayer of thanksgiving for Bert's life, then said a blessing for those who carried on after him.

Once the service was complete his uncle's peers gathered around, introduced themselves and spoke of the man they'd loved. Though Daniel couldn't remember their names, each offered some individual insight into his uncle that reminded Daniel that not only he had lost a loved one. These men were also mourning.

Then they moved to the garden at the back of the church, where a small plot had been prepared. Without fuss or frills Bert was laid to rest among others of God's children. Then the gathering dissipated until only Daniel and Samantha were left standing there.

Samantha's hand crept into his. "He's at home now, Daniel. He's happy."

"I know." He reached into his pocket, took out the handful of lemon drops he'd brought when he'd arrived, back when he still hoped to have a visit with his uncle. Raising his hand, he dropped them, winced at the *plink* they made against the casket. "Goodbye," he whispered.

Together they left the garden, passed through the dim interior of the church and emerged into the blazing sun, blinking furiously.

"Look!" Sam murmured.

Hundreds of people had gathered around the outside of the church holding flowers—white orchids—and candles. They said nothing, but many had their eyes closed and their lips were moving as if they were in prayer.

As if his appearance was a signal, they formed a line and one by one began dropping their flowers in front of a huge wreath someone had placed in the center of the steps, which bore a simple ribbon and the word *Padre-cito*—beloved priest. Silently they nodded at him, then walked away.

Daniel knew they had less than an hour to get to the Inca Museum if they were to learn any more about the statue. But Daniel couldn't—wouldn't—leave until everyone had a chance to pay their respects. When the last flower had been laid, the last person gone, he took a deep breath and unashamedly wiped the tears from his eyes.

"That was quite a tribute," Sam murmured. "I had no idea so many people knew him."

"Uncle Bert worked at a mission here in the city when he was young." He matched her steps down. "He often stopped by when he was in Lima, just to see old friends and say hello. I guess they wanted to do the same today."

They climbed into a cab and headed across the city to the Inca Museum, a silent ride filled with thoughts too personal to discuss.

"According to that sign, the museum is closed," Sam said, waiting for him to pay the cabbie.

"Probably because Sanchez knows we're coming." He pushed the door open as if to prove his point. Somewhere inside a buzzer sounded and seconds later Sanchez came rushing toward them.

"Hola, mis amigos." He stood in front of them so they could not enter the museum proper. "I have good news."

"You've found the statue?" Sam asked, her disbelief obvious.

"A letter was waiting when I arrived. The statue is to be delivered in just a few minutes. But I warn you, Ms. Henderson. I will not sell it. I have already had my bank transfer the money. The statue will be part of my personal collection."

"Who had it?" The niggle on Daniel's neck was getting stronger with every second he stood there. He took Samantha's hand. "I think we should come back tomorrow and talk about this."

"Why? We're here now. I want to wait for the statue." She glanced out the picture window. "So tell us."

Daniel followed her gaze. A long black car slid along the curb. No one got out. More niggling.

"I received a phone call telling me that if I was interested in the statue I should send money to a certain address." He held out a slip of paper. "I did that and—" Sanchez froze. His mouth stayed open, his eyes never moved but he fell forward.

As Daniel yanked Sam back, he stared at the small round hole in the man's head. Without thinking, he pulled open the door and shoved her onto the sidewalk, checking over his shoulder to see if they were followed.

"Someone shot him, Daniel." Her shock was obvious.

"Yes. Did you see anything? Anyone?"

She shook her head, mute though her eyes spoke volumes.

"I've got to get that policeman. Stay put. Don't let anyone in, okay?" He cupped her face in his hands. "Did you hear me, Sam?"

"Yes. Go. I'll be fine." She half turned toward the door as if to protect it from intruders.

The uniformed cop was about to turn the corner. Daniel raised his hand, ready to yell, when a hand grabbed his arm.

"Excuse me, *señor?*"

"Yes?" He half turned then lost his balance as someone shoved him from behind. He fell into the back of a car. Seconds later the vehicle sped down the street, away from Samantha.

TWELVE

Where was Daniel?

Exhausted by the repeated questions from police, Sam greeted the sight of her old friend Jose Rodriguez with delight. He listened as she told the story once more then said something to the other cops. They frowned but apparently agreed to whatever he said.

"This officer will take you back to your hotel," he told her. "If we need anything more I'll call you, okay?"

"More than okay. Thank you very much." She got in the car.

"Just one thing before you go," he said, leaning in to look at her. "Why were you at the Inca Museum after hours? Something to do with Finders, Inc., I assume?"

"A statue that was stolen." She filled him in on the details. "Sanchez said he'd paid for it, that it was supposed to arrive any moment. He had a bit of paper in his hand—maybe the delivery company?"

"Okay, I'll get someone to hang around in case anything is delivered."

"Thanks, Jose. I really appreciate this."

"Just remember that if you run into something big, let me know. With another baby on the way, I'm hoping for a promotion. But it takes a lot to impress my boss."

"If I get something, I promise I'll call." She hadn't mentioned Daniel to any of the others and she didn't tell Jose, either. Now was not the time to put out a missing persons bulletin. She needed to talk to Shelby first.

At the hotel, Samantha hurried up to her room, stepped inside and locked the door behind her and drew a deep breath. Safe at last. She jumped as her phone began to ring.

"Samantha? Shelby. Do you know where Daniel is? I've been trying to reach him but his phone's off."

In a rush of words Sam poured out her story. "All I can think is that we got too close."

"They took only Daniel, not you. I think that means they're going to call you, ask for something. Someone's been asking you for 'merchandise.' Maybe you'll finally find out what that means."

"I guess."

"All you can do is wait for someone to contact you. But in the meantime, you'd better check your e-mail. Daniel asked me to look into something. I think we found what he was looking for. Go ahead, I'll wait."

"It's dial-up, Shelby. It'll take me a few minutes. Besides, I don't want to tie up the line. I'll call you back after I take a look."

"Okay. Keep the faith, Sam. God's got it all under control."

"Uh-huh." Sam wasn't so sure. She opened Daniel's laptop, connected and checked her e-mail. She clicked on the attachment, fingers tapping restlessly against the tabletop as it loaded.

The pictures puzzled her and she wondered why Daniel had wanted a full-color spread from a newspaper with a write-up about the theft of the statue and the museum that was to receive it. Sam scrolled down the columns, found nothing of interest there. She went back up and zoomed in on the pictures one by one.

There were several of the museum in Rio, and she studied each one. She felt a numbing chill when she got to the third and saw Ric—in a courier's outfit, standing beside a delivery truck. One shot frozen in time, yet it said everything. Like tumblers in a lock, the pieces clicked together.

Daniel had suspected Ric for some time. He'd probably seen this article as part of the research file and recalled it after meeting Ric. A courier would be able to find out the route the statue would take, learn every stop, every check- in point, know exactly where to look.

It was too much of a coincidence that Ric just happened to be at the museum the day after the theft of this particular statue. It was probably too much of a coincidence that he'd appeared in South America just as she began a new assignment to find the same statue.

Her phone pealed again.

"Shelby, I'm not sure—"

"All will be clear, Ms. Henderson. Just listen." A man's voice, soft but threaded with steel.

"I'm listening." She gripped the handset tightly, waited.

"I have your boyfriend."

"Daniel? Is he all right? What do you want?"

"You may recall an incident in the jungle recently." He paused. "A priest took something of mine. I want it back."

"And you think I have it?" Icy fingers touched her spine. She was talking to Father Bert's killer.

"That is my information."

"Then your information is wrong. I have no idea what you're talking about."

"That is sad, Ms. Henderson. Because it will cost your friend his life."

"Wait!" She held her breath until she was sure he was still there. "I don't think you're talking about the statue, are you?" An epithet. "All right, just checking. So what are we talking about?" Utter silence. Sam bit her lip, then plunged ahead, hoping what she did now wouldn't affect Daniel adversely. "Look, buddy, I'm good at retrievals, but if you want me to find something you have to at least give me a clue. What am I looking for?"

A long pause. Then, "Six kilos wrapped in clear plastic, worth over five-hundred-thousand American dollars."

Drugs. Probably cocaine.

Ric had been investigating drugs. "Okay. I understand. Now let me talk to Daniel."

"Thanks, Carlos. Samantha?"

That voice—she closed her eyes, breathed. "Are you all right?"

"Samantha." He sounded hoarse. "It's good to hear your voice, honey."

Honey? Back to role-playing, which meant he was trying to tell her something. She grabbed a pencil ready to take notes.

"Listen, sweetheart. I want you to find us a place in Lima where we can settle down and let the world pass by. A nice little bungalow where we can hide from the world and spend our coins. Talk to Shelby. Ask her to look up suitable places where we'll fit in. Can you do that?"

"Yes. Got it."

"I love you, Samantha."

"So sweet." The acid tones of the kidnapper cut in. "You do not have much time, Ms. Henderson. I will call you tomorrow afternoon at five o'clock. If you've found my merchandise your *novio* will return safe and sound."

"I need more time than that!"

"Five o'clock. Do not cross me or you will wish you have never come to Peru. *Adios.*"

After Sam closed her phone, she stared at what she'd written then dialed Finders. "Shelby? I just heard from Daniel. Someone named Carlos is holding him. I'm pretty sure it's Carlos Velázquez. He wants me to find his merchandise—I think it's cocaine. Six kilos."

"What do you know of this man, Sam?" Shelby sounded worried.

"He's a top gun among the drug bosses down here. Not to be messed with. Very nasty. At least that's the talk on the street."

"So if you ever want to work in South America again, you've got to get him off your tail, right?"

"Yes. I'm wondering if he's also called el Zopilote?"

"The Vulture? Not that I've seen, but I'll take another look. We've been trying but haven't been able to track that name down. What did Daniel say?"

Samantha blushed as she recited the message. "It's a game we played on the cruise ship. He doesn't mean anything by it."

"You know that isn't true." Shelby's voice came back, soft but firm. "Daniel means everything he says. That's what makes him one of the good guys. Now tell me what you want me to do."

"The only person I know that I can connect to drugs is Ric Preston—he was supposedly investigating them. That's his picture in the newspaper article you sent so we'll start there. You already did some research on him for Daniel. E-mail me that and every other single bit of information you can find on him ASAP. Include anything interesting in any of the South American papers."

"Done."

Sam reviewed her notes. "I think Daniel was trying to tell me to ask you to find out something, but I'm not sure what. I'll work on that. Get back to me fast, Shelby. This could be life or death."

"I'll put everyone on it. I'll also be praying, Sam."

"Thanks." Samantha closed the phone. Life or death made her blood run cold. Daniel couldn't die. She didn't want to think it, but the reality was that it could happen if she didn't stop it. But she needed help.

Daniel's Bible lay on the table. Sam picked it up, leafed through the pages. "What am I supposed to do?" She glanced down, saw the section she'd read this morning on the cruise.

> We are pressed on every side by troubles, but not crushed and broken. We are perplexed because we don't know why things happen as they do, but we don't give up. We are hunted down, but God never abandons us. We get knocked down but we get up again and keep going.

That was her. Pressed on every side, perplexed, hunted down.

But God never abandons us.

If only she could believe that.

Daniel claimed she'd lost the promotion because she didn't work cooperatively. But she was alone now. She didn't dare trust Ric and Shelby was too far away. So…

"I need help, God," she admitted. The relief of finally

admitting it made it easier to press on. "If You do love me," she whispered, "please show me what to do. I'm so tired of trying to manage on my own."

The silent enemy crouched inside her heart finally showed his face as her fear inflated. What if God didn't care, what if she'd lost her chance, what if—decision time!

Either she trusted in God here and now or she turned her back once and for all. Nobody could sit on the fence forever, but to trust meant depending on someone else, something she hated to do. The battle raged in her heart, till her soul cried out for peace. Pretending she could stand alone—that was a lie. She wanted the simple faith of her childhood back, longed to experience again the certainty that she was loved. The first step was up to her.

Taking a deep breath of courage, she squeezed her eyes closed and made a promise. "I'll trust You."

There was no sudden rush of feeling, no freedom from the trials she'd fallen into. Just the calm, steady certainty that she was no longer alone. God would take care of her. She was His beloved child.

Her phone rang.

"Found something that's going to blow your socks off, Sam. Check your e-mail. Bye."

Surprised by Shelby's excitement, Samantha clicked on the icon and began to read the attachment—a newspaper article from two years ago.

Friends and family say goodbye to Maria Gonzales, 24, today at the church of San Francisco, Lima, Peru. Gonzales had ties to the Solidad smuggling operation recently broken up by police. Details of her part in the operation have yet to be released but police suspect she was killed as repayment for drugs the smugglers had accidentally taken from a local cartel.

Samantha rose on shaky legs and let her mind replay the details of that case—her case. Back then she'd tracked a diamond bracelet to Maria. Once she'd uncovered ties to the notorious Solidad smugglers, Sam had called in Interpol.

She scanned the rest of the piece, honed in on the notation at the bottom. Gonzales is survived by her loving husband Ricardo. She fit the pieces together. Ricardo and Maria Gonzales. Ric Preston?

A sound at the door stopped all thought. Samantha crept to one side of it, waited. The knock came again. *"Es el botones. Tengo una carta para usted."* The bellboy had a letter. Was it another trick?

She opened the door a crack. A young man was holding out a tray on which rested a brown puffy envelope marked Urgent. Sam took it and closed the door. From Finders. She tore it open, saw Shelby's handwriting. *Thought you should have this now.*

A thin white letter slid out of the envelope, addressed to Daniel. The sender was his uncle, the postmark before Bert's death.

Sam held it for a moment, then made her decision. If there was something inside that could help, Daniel would want her to read it. She slit the thin envelope and read the words. Then she grabbed her phone.

"Shelby, I just got Daniel's letter from his uncle and I read it. Listen. Bert thought someone was using his plane trips to transport drugs or guns from Colombia along with the supplies he brought in. He was going to ask Finders for help."

"Did he name anyone as a suspect?"

"He talks about a new friend." Sam scanned the writing again. "Bert doesn't identify him but says he's concerned that the man's primary interest isn't in bringing medical supplies into the compound. He talks about a bequest he's passing on to Daniel and asks him to meet in Lima."

"What bequest would a priest leave?"

"The coins, of course." Suddenly the pieces were sliding together faster than she could fit them. "New job for you guys at Finders. Go through the newspapers, Interpol, customs and border notices, anything like that. See if you can find something that talks about gold or coins being recently sold to a museum or the Peruvian government. I'll do the same here. It's important, Shelby."

"Daniel asked about gold earlier. We didn't find anything but we'll try again. All of the Finders, Inc. resources have been directed to this case. Grant may be gone but I refuse to lose Daniel, too," Shelby said, her tone grim. "If there's anything else, phone me. I'll be here all night."

"I won't. I'm going out. On a date." Her notes from Daniel's call were lying on the table. Samantha read them again. Suddenly she knew exa[illegible]t to do. "One other thing. Do a search on prop[illegible] See if you can find a residential lot or [illegible] Gonzales or Ric Preston as the liste[illegible] precedes the other. I've got to kn[illegible]

"We'll do what we can. Be ca[illegible] guys aren't fooling."

"Neither am I," she promis[illegible] button again and dialed the [illegible] the day she'd left the jung[illegible] shortly after the bus had dropped her off. Her knight in shining armor—or so he'd seemed.

“Hi, Ric. Listen, I'm frustrated and fed up and I need to get out of this hotel. Want to meet me somewhere?”

“You're not a drinker so I'm guessing a bar won't do it. How about Barranco? There are usually things going on till all hours in that neighborhood.”

“Sounds wonderful,” she said, knowing the heart of the city's contemporary arts and nightlife center was probably the safest place for her to be right now. “Just what I need. I'll meet you in front of the fountain as soon as I can get there, okay?”

When he'd agreed, Samantha hung up. She gathered all her notes and the laptop and tucked them away under the bed, just in case. When the room was tidy she changed clothes and went downstairs. The bellboy blinked at her.

“I'm sorry I was in such a rush earlier,” she apologized, sliding a tip into his hand. “Can you get me a taxi?”

Thirty minutes later she was stepping out of her taxi in the midst of Lima's busy night scene. Ric bounded over to meet her, his face creased in a wide grin. “This is a pleasure,” he said as he hugged her. “I thought you'd be with your boss. Nothing wrong, is there?”

She made a face. “With Daniel there's always something wrong. I don't want to talk about him or business or anything else. Tonight I just want to relax and enjoy Lima. Can we do that?”

“Sure.” For the next three hours they listened to folk ...ming from the *peñas*. After a while it changed ...reole, a combination of European music ...n, Spanish and African rhythms and ...idst the gorgeous nineteenth-century architecture, murder and drug runners seemed a dream. When the celebration grew too rowdy, Ric coaxed her to visit his favorite restaurant in Miraflores where they watched live theater while eating.

Samantha found the meal difficult as her stomach twisted with nerves. Ric, on the other hand, had no problem devouring his marinated grilled beef heart. When at last they were finished, she sipped her coffee and tried not to show her impatience at his poorly disguised probing.

"I couldn't have asked for a better evening, Ric," she told him when they finally left the restaurant. "Thank you so much."

"It doesn't have to end now," he hinted with a wink.

"Yes, it does. Finders will be calling bright and early tomorrow morning and my boss is going to be pretty upset when I tell her Daniel—no, never mind." She leaned forward, bussed his cheek. "Thank you."

"Anytime, Sam. You know that." He called her a cab, handed her in and waited till it pulled away. Then he hailed one for himself.

"Change of plan," she told her driver. "Follow him, please. But don't make it obvious."

They followed Ric to a newer part of the Miraflores district, slowing as they climbed up a hill. A pretty house stood at the top. Ric entered it, turned on the lights. Samantha noted the address on a piece of paper then directed the driver to take her back to the hotel.

Inside her room she first ensured no one had visited in her absence, then set up the computer and began an Internet search that lasted over an hour. By then Shelby was on the line.

"Lima has most of their newer properties online. We're still searching."

"Concentrate on the Miraflores area. Anything on the coins or gold front?"

"Still working on that. Why don't you get some rest?"

"In a while. Thanks, Shelby."

When there was nothing more she could do, Samantha lay on the bed, but she couldn't sleep. Instead she went over and over her plan, searching for a flaw that would upset things.

Or worse—one that would put Daniel in more danger than he already was.

It was like being locked in isolation. No one to talk to, no outside stimulus, no pain to agonize over, nothing but utter darkness and silence.

Daniel lay on his bed in the pitch-black room and tried to recall a hymn, a sermon he'd heard, something that would remind him that God was here, in this place.

We are perplexed because we don't understand why things happen as they do, but we don't give up. We are hunted down but God never abandons us.

He repeated it to himself. "God never abandons us."

He drew a deep, calming breath as the words sank to his soul and rested there. God would be with Samantha, too. He could picture her—the rich emerald of her eyes, how they darkened and glittered when she was mad at him. He could hear her voice—trying to comfort him, sassing him just to get a rise, full of awe and reverence when she spoke of Uncle Bert.

If only she'd understood his message. Not about Ric. Sam was smart enough to figure that out on her own.

But had she believed him when he said he loved her?

Not likely. Daniel faced reality. When it concerned him, Sam usually needed convincing. He longed to do that, to be there to tell and show her what lay in his heart. He wanted to coax her to have faith in him, bit by bit, until it was as solid and strong a bond as any two people could form.

But beyond his own longings, Daniel wanted her to know and understand the power and depth of God's love for her. He wanted her to know the joy and freedom of trusting in the only One who would never disappoint, never leave, never betray.

"Let her find You," he whispered over and over. "Open her eyes, show her You are not the enemy but the truest friend she'll ever have."

He wanted so much to be a part of the rest of her life, but as he lay in his narrow cot in this black, oppressive room, Daniel knew it was unlikely he'd ever see Samantha again. It was well-known that Carlos Velázquez had never released anyone who'd been brought to this place. No wonder it was called *la casa de la muerte,* the house of death. The stench of evil hung on the air, infiltrated the thick adobe walls.

"I'm ready to die, Lord," he murmured. "If that is Your will, so be it. Only let Samantha be safe."

No response. Isolated from everyone.

Except God.

THIRTEEN

The telephone rang at 9:43 a.m. Samantha jumped out of bed and grabbed it, trying to come awake. "Hello?"

"We found it!" Shelby said triumphantly. "A transaction was made by the Gold Museum almost three weeks ago. The government of Peru agreed to the conditions and terms stipulated by one Berton McCullough. I've e-mailed you a copy."

"Great! And the property?"

"Nothing. I'm sorry, Samantha. I've tried everything I can think of."

Her heart sank. She had to find that cocaine. Without it Daniel was a dead man. *Think.* Every *i* dotted, every *t* crossed. That's the way Finders, Inc. had kept its reputation. No loose ends—Daniel had taught her that. She had to tie this up so that when she left the company no one would have to justify her work.

The notepad lay on the table. Samantha grabbed a pencil and began to doodle, begging her brain to yield just one more answer to the puzzle. Her fingers froze as she stared at the word.

"Try searching once more, Shelby."

"Sam, you know we've—"

"Please. Just once more. Plug in el Zopilote and see what you come up with using it and any other variations you can think of."

"The Vulture? Okay, we'll give it a shot."

"I'd also like somebody to find out who the owner of this address is." She read the numbers she'd scrawled down last night. Ric wouldn't use his main address, would he?

"No problem."

"And Shelby?"

"Yes?"

"We haven't got much time left."

"I know."

Everything else fit. This would, too. It was the last bit.

"I know it off by heart now," she said, grinning as the verse from Daniel's Bible beamed up at her. "Pressed but not crushed and broken, perplexed but not giving up, hunted down but not abandoned. Got it, God."

Samantha showered quickly, pulled on her jeans and an old T-shirt. Her sneakers had seen better days but she didn't even bother to try and clean them. She checked to be sure her purse held her phone and sunglasses, then zipped it closed. Then she looked at herself in the mirror.

An ordinary, garden-variety tourist. After a quick breakfast at a sidewalk café, Sam set out searching for Bertha-the-street-lady. She wasn't sitting at either of her favorite spots and for a moment Sam almost panicked.

"We are pressed on every side," she muttered as she checked alleys and walks. At last she found the woman in Plaza des Armas sitting on a park bench.

"*Hola,* Bertha."

Bertha smiled then began to gripe about Sam's shorn head.

"I'll tell you why I did it sometime. But this morning I need a favor. Do you know of el Padre Dulce?" Bertha nodded, her face sad. "I'm trying to help his nephew bring el Padre's killer to justice but I can't do it alone. I've got a plan but I need a diversion." She explained her idea carefully. Bertha began to grin and didn't stop until Sam was finished. "Will you help me?"

"Sí. Yo le ayudaré y mis amigos, también." I'll help you. My friends also.

"Thank you. This is what I need you to do." She explained, made sure the woman understood. "It has to look like you're supposed to be there," she warned.

"No preocupe. Cuidaré de todo." Don't worry, I'll take care of everything. *"Para el Padrecito."* For our dear father.

At one she met Bertha's helpers and told them her plan. Assured they would not let her down, Sam returned to her hotel to wait. Shelby called a half hour after that.

"The property at the address you gave me is owned by Señor and Señora Zopilote."

Samantha closed her eyes as the words sank in.

"Sam?"

"I'm here. Thanks, Shelby. That's what I needed."

"Anything more I can do?"

"Pray, because there's no way I can pull this off on my own."

They were moving him.

Daniel tried to absorb sounds, discern what they meant, but he never had a chance before he was thrust into an armchair and told to wait. A few moments later his blindfold was removed.

He blinked at the opulence surrounding him. To the left the Pacific sparkled in the dazzling sun. To the right lay an azure pool filled with children laughing and giggling. Something was happening.

"We will phone your true love now, *señor.* Let us hope she has lived up to her reputation, hmm?" Carlos Velázquez dialed, waited, one perfectly polished Brazilian leather shoe tapping against the marble floor. When he got no response, he swore, clicked the phone off, and then dialed again, his mouth a thin straight line. "Ah, *señorita.* How kind of you to answer?"

"Sorry. I was in the shower." Sam's clear voice carried to Daniel. She sounded sassy, defiant.

Don't bait him, he wanted to yell. But that wouldn't help.

"Do you have my merchandise?"

"I'm prepared to make you a trade, *señor.* Your, er, merchandise for Daniel."

"No deals, *señorita.*" Carlos's eyes grew hard, cold.

"Then no cocaine. And you will never know of the silent enemy you have in your midst." A faint click.

Daniel leaned forward. Surely she hadn't hung up? Carlos, too, seemed stunned. His eyes blazed with fury and his body stiffened. He slammed the phone down into its cradle and glared at it.

"Well, you did ask her to find the stuff," Daniel sputtered. "I guess she found more than you imagined. After all, she is the best."

"There is no enemy in my organization. My people are loyal."

"Then how did your packages go missing?"

Carlos said nothing, but finally he dialed again. Daniel tried not to show his relief.

"You have my attention, Ms. Henderson."

"I want to speak to Daniel."

"It is not—"

She must have hung up again. Inwardly Daniel was groaning at her temerity, but part of him couldn't help admiring her spunk. Who else would take on a drug lord?

For the third time Carlos dialed the number, but this time he handed the phone to Daniel.

"Samantha? It's me."

"Are you all right?"

"Yes." Silence. "Sam?"

"I'm here. Tell Carlos he is to meet me at the Church of San Francisco. I'm sure he knows where it is. You and him, nobody else, no guns. Seven o'clock. If I see anything funny, he won't see his stuff."

Daniel glanced up, wondering if Carlos had heard it all. He had and it infuriated him.

"Okay, he knows."

"There's more than one person involved in this exposé, Daniel, so you and Carlos will have to stay where you're told. Don't move, don't say a word until I tell you to. Got it?"

"Yes." He licked his lips. "Are you sure about this, Samantha?"

"Trust me."

His heart soared. She'd asked the hardest thing of him, the only thing he couldn't use his money to get. The only thing that mattered.

"I trust you, Samantha. And I love you."

"Me, too." Another lapse. Then, "Put Carlos on."

He handed the phone back.

Daniel heard nothing else. He was too busy trying to absorb the meaning of those two words. *Me, too.*

Samantha Henderson loved him—since when?

Daniel's reverie was shattered as Carlos's men shoved the blindfold over his eyes and grabbed him by his arms, forcing him out of the room. A few minutes later he was back in his cell.

"Make it work, Lord. Please make Sam's plan work, because I can't die now. Not now."

Samantha walked up the path to the front door. It was thrown open before she got there. Bertha stood in the doorway, her mouth stretched in a comical grin.

"*Hola, señorita.* The *señor,* he is most appreciative that a plumber and a maid should be in the neighborhood. There is much disaster when broken pipes must be mended." She spread her arms wide. "Everything is neat and clean, no mess at all."

"You didn't find it."

"No." Bertha shook her head sadly. "I'm sorry."

Samantha closed her eyes as the weight of what she'd done hit home. Daniel's life was at stake. But she'd been so sure—

"What's behind that fence?"

"The gardening shed. The *señor* has a fountain and many flowers. There is a little plaque, too. It says Maria."

A glimmer of hope returned. "Show me."

The garden was a riot of vivid color and bursting life, obviously a place that received tender care. A stone wall surrounded a fountain on three sides.

"An odd structure, is it not? I don't understand the way it is built."

"Nor do I." Sam removed several pots of flowers to get a better look. She used her fingers to probe the bricks from behind and at last found a small opening at the very back of the structure. She moved more pots, managed to squeeze in behind, felt the hard metal corners of—a chest? "Help me, please."

Together she and Bertha worked it free of its hiding place, pulled it into the light. It looked like the chest from the jungle, but there was no way to be certain. Until she saw the initials BM on the brass hasp.

"Don't touch it," she ordered Bertha as she pulled out her phone and dialed. "Jose? You know that promotion you talked about? I think I might have a way you can earn it. Can you come right away?" She gave him the address, had barely hung up the phone when it rang again.

"The *señor* is coming home now. It seems there was a mistake. He is not urgently needed at the police station after all."

"How long?" Sam demanded.

"He has a flat tire on his car. Perhaps an hour."

"Thank you, Tomas. You're a son to be proud of. Bertha is leaving now." Amidst the woman's protests Sam sent her off with her plumber friend. "Go to the Plaza, find a place near the church and wait. I'll come as soon as I can."

They'd barely left before Jose pulled up, siren screaming. So much for covert operations.

"I'm missing a very important briefing," he told her. "I hope this is worthwhile."

"Come and see." As they went, she told him her story. "I haven't opened it or done anything to it. I thought you should be a witness to that."

"You broke in here?"

"No. I didn't go inside, didn't want to trespass. I came to see a friend who was working here. She showed me the garden and I was exploring it." She kept her face deadpan.

"*Ay-yi-yi.*" He shook his head at her, fiddled with the lock. "I don't suppose you have the key?" When she shook her head, he nodded. "Very well. I'll try to open it." He picked up a rock but Sam stopped him.

"This might work," she murmured holding out a lock pick.

He gave her a look that needed no translation then bent and worked the lock free of the trunk. He lifted the lid.

"*¡Cielos!* What is this?"

"Cocaine, I think." She waited while he made a tiny hole in the bag, tasted it, then nodded. "I'm pretty sure it belongs to Carlos Velázquez." With great care she lifted out the packets until she could see beneath. Coins, hundreds of them, filled the rest of the trunk. "Those belonged to el Padre Dulce. They were stolen from him the day he was murdered." As quickly as she could, she explained her plan. "If you hear them confess you can arrest all of them. I'll be your witness, so will Daniel. That should get you a promotion to head of the police force."

"It is very dangerous to do such a thing to Carlos, Samantha."

"It's also the only way I can think of to bring those who are responsible for murder, theft and drug smuggling to justice. Will you help me?"

She needed him on her side. Otherwise she would no doubt run into problems. Carlos Velázquez had friends in high places.

"Explain it to me again."

She laid it out, step by step. "But we have to hurry. The man who lives here is on his way and we must be gone before that."

Jose stared at the cocaine for a long time. Finally he nodded.

"Good. You know what to do with that, right? You'll go directly to the church? Carlos has to see it or he'll kill Daniel."

Jose nodded, grinned. "If this succeeds and I get a raise, I will name our next child after you."

"The highest honor." She helped him load the chest in his car, and then returned the garden to its original state. After that Sam rode with Jose to the nearest taxi stand where she got out. She paused to make two more calls.

Now everything was in place. It was time to face the enemy.

FOURTEEN

"Plaza des Armas, often called Plaza Mayor, is the main square in Lima. It was declared a world heritage site by UNESCO. Bullfights were held there before the Plaza de Acho bullring was built in 1766. Since that time the people of Peru have changed their country magnificently."

Samantha stepped around the tour group and crossed the cobbled pavers searching the plaza for Bertha and her group. A gardener worked on one of the flower beds on the north end of the Plaza beside the Government Palace, but he was pulling out more plants than weeds. Bertha's son Tomas, no doubt.

Running along two sides of the plaza were Portal de Escribanos and Portal de Botoneros. Both streets were littered with arcades and shops and curious tourists. Bertha had set up shop on one corner, her handmade trinkets displayed on a brightly colored shawl.

To the east of the Plaza sat the Cathedral of the city of Lima with its twin bright yellow bell towers. The plumber and his protégé were hawking flowers from their cart. On the west side lay the Municipalidad de Lima, residence of the city's mayor. Arches on the first and second floor shadowed the front, a perfect spot for someone to hide in. Hopefully one of the good guys was there.

Samantha shivered, forcing herself to walk steadily forward. For someone Daniel said wasn't good with cooperation, she had the biggest joint venture happening right in this square. She'd remind him of that irony later, when he was safe.

Someone bumped into her. She stumbled slightly until a hand appeared on her arm, steadied her.

"Everything is ready. I have men all over. They don't know why they are here but no one will move until I say so." Jose pointed as if he were asking directions. "Find the garden of the monastery. Wait there. The others will be directed to it when they arrive at the church."

"Okay."

"Sí. Muchas gracias, señorita." Jose walked over to a nearby bench, sat down beside a flower bed filled with brilliant red bird of paradise and pulled out a book.

A flurry of activity in front of the palace signaled the changing of the guard. Samantha used the opportunity to take stock of the crowd. Red-coated soldiers wearing blue pants tucked into long black boots stomped and marched their way across the plaza in front of the palace. Each blue hat was perched at exactly the same angle, red tops inclined just so. But she couldn't identify even one as a real policeman. Good.

Sam stopped at the stone facade of the Church of San Francisco, mingled with a tour group entering the church. She was early, but she needed to familiarize herself with the scene. She could leave nothing to chance.

The magnificent Moorish-style carved wood ceilings

soared upward while Spanish tiles decorated other areas. She'd been here before and knew the colonial-era church dated from 1674. To her mind it had lost none of its beauty in centuries since. A reverence she couldn't explain filled her as she stared down the long aisle to the altar in front.

Others slipped into pews. The sanctuary fell silent. Sam walked forward until she was near enough to look into the eyes of the man who hung on a wooden cross. Someone had placed a banner at His feet, a plain length of cloth with letters painted on, not the finest of cloth but its message overrode any simplicity.

I love you.

Tears welled in her eyes at this confirmation that she was not alone, that God was here. Whatever happened now it was up to Him. She hoped Daniel felt that same assurance. Maybe it would help him to trust her.

She checked her watch, then left the sanctuary.

The garden of the monastery formed a crisscross of walkways intersected by soft, cascading fountains, blooming camellias and a surrounding colonnade of white stone pillars that offered a sense of security from the world beyond. It was peaceful, certainly not a place where one would expect to find evil lurking.

Samantha chose a spot beside a lemon tree and waited. She heard a soft rustle then two men appeared. Seconds later another behind them.

"Gentlemen, please come in." She stared into the eyes of Bert's murderer and refused to flinch. "Señor Velázquez, I assume. Please sit over there. You're all right?" she asked Daniel, allowing herself a few seconds to soak in the sight of his face as a rush of joy suffused her heart.

"I'm fine, Samantha. Thank you." He stared at her as if he were thirsty. Samantha smiled. *Thank you, Lord.*

"If you wouldn't mind sitting beside Señor Velázquez, Daniel. Just for the time being. Señor Obrigado, you may sit here. Thank you."

"*Señorita,* please explain what this is about." Obrigado rose, moved as if to come toward her, but she held up a hand.

"Sit down, *señor.* Please. I have a story to tell you." She waited until the other man had complied, then bent and moved a big flowering pot to reveal the chest. "My story concerns this chest. It belonged to a man named Bert McCullough. It was something he cherished for many years because a friend made it for him. He told his nephew that one day it would be filled with the treasure. He was right."

"My patience is thin, *señorita.* I—"

"Be quiet," she ordered. "You will hear me out."

Velázquez held up his hands and shrugged as if placating her, but Sam saw the glitter of anger in those dark eyes and hurried on.

"I'll continue. Every year Bert would return to a certain location to dive for this treasure. One year he finally kept his promise to his nephew. He found his treasure and he kept it in this very chest. Golden coins worth a fortune."

The bored looks were gone. Behind the men, bougainvillea blossoms shuddered. Sam caught a glimpse of Ric standing at the edge of the garden. Jose had moved behind him, still out of sight but at the ready.

"Perhaps you'd like to join us, Ric," she offered quietly. "We're talking about truth."

"I don't think you have anything to say that's of

interest to me," he denied, but his voice choked when he saw the chest.

"Have a seat anyway." Sam continued. "The coins came from a sunken ship off the coast of Peru, the *Isadora.* But then you know all this, don't you, gentlemen?"

"It's a very curious story." Velázquez glanced at the others. "I do not understand how it interests me however."

"Patience, Señor Velázquez. You will." Sam cleared her throat. "As a missionary, Bert cared deeply for the people of Peru. He spent his life teaching them about God. He hired someone to fly a plane so he could transport in supplies to the natives he worked with along the Amazon."

"Samantha, I really wish you hadn't called me in for this. I'm working on a case." Ric shrugged.

"About drugs. I know. I think you'll see the connection in a moment." She met Daniel's gaze, smiled. "Bert wrote a letter to his nephew before he died in which he said someone was using his supply trips to transport drugs or perhaps guns from Colombia into his mission compound. He suspected a new 'friend' who claimed to want to help him with his work."

"Señorita Henderson—"

"Do me the courtesy of listening, Señor Velázquez." She glared at him, incensed by the outrage he'd committed. He clamped his lips together. Sam raised her arm and pointed. "Bert's friend was you, Ric."

"Come on, Sam." Ric smirked. "I was sent to find out who was transporting the stuff. I tracked it and fingered Bert."

"I think it was the other way around—he fingered you." Sam opened the trunk, revealing the plastic-wrapped packages. "My guess is you were hired to move the drugs to a distribution point. I'm sure you were well paid for your efforts. I wonder why that wasn't enough for you."

Velázquez cleared his throat, his eyes shooting daggers at Ric who blustered into speech.

"This is crazy. I'm CIA. Why would I want to deal in cocaine?"

Sam stared at him. "Who said it was cocaine, Ric?"

To his credit he never flinched under her glare. "That's what I've been tracking. I naturally assumed—"

"You assumed a lot." Samantha let her disdain show. "You assumed Varga would keep doing your bidding and when you heard he'd talked to me that night on the cruise, you had him killed. You assumed Señor Velázquez wouldn't mind giving up some of his product every time you handled it. You assumed nobody would uncover your little scheme or hold you accountable. You assumed you could use me to maintain your house of lies until Carlos here killed me or Daniel, or both of us."

"This is nuts. You should have her committed," he said to Daniel.

"Or promoted." Daniel sat back, crossed his arms over his chest. "Please continue, Samantha."

She was sick of the lies. "Did you or did you not offer to fly Bert's plane for him, Ric?"

"Of course. That was all part of the cover."

She nodded. "The cover to set me up. It began with the statue." She smiled at Obrigado's surprise. "He stole it, and then offered to sell it to Sanchez. Knowing such an Inca treasure was available, Eduardo Sanchez jumped at the opportunity. When he heard I was tracking Varga because he was supposed to have it, he tried to make his own deal."

"Varga's statue was never real," Obrigado butted in.

"It didn't need to be. Ric knew South America was my field, that Finders, Inc. would send me after the statue, which so conveniently turned up in Lima. Ric hired Varga to keep me busy. The plan was to get me into the jungle."

Velázquez couldn't take his eyes off the drugs. "Why?"

"He needed a patsy." She turned on Ric. "Bert told you about the coins, didn't he? You were probably with him when he took them to Lima to arrange some kind of settlement with the government."

"The government of Peru knows of no coins," Obrigado began but Sam merely laughed.

"Your name is on the agreement, *señor.* Half of the coins went to the Gold Museum here, the other half were Bert's to keep. Only you wanted them."

"It is a sacrilege to let our national treasures be removed from this country," Obrigado said, his lips drawn in a snarl. "This is our heritage."

"They're Spanish, not Peruvian," she reminded him. "You have no right to them. But you decided to go after them anyway. That's where our buddy Ric comes in."

"Really, Samantha, this is foolish."

"Is it?" Sam turned her attention to Velázquez. "You ordered Bert shot because he wouldn't return your drugs. You killed an innocent man. He never had your cocaine. Neither did I."

"But I was told—"

"By Ric, am I right?" Sam saw Carlos incline his head. "You probably never saw his face while you were in the jungle, never even knew he was there, but Ric knew every move we made. He orchestrated it all."

"Why?" Velázquez shot Ric a deadly glare.

"So he could take the cocaine. He told you I had it, didn't he? Or he hinted that I might know how to get it?" She smiled at his hesitation. "It was no accident that he agreed to run your dope, to endanger himself. Ric Preston was a man on a mission."

"This is stupid. What possible reason—"

"You see, *señor,* the plan was to avenge his wife's death, Maria Gonzales. A death he blamed you for. She was the reason for all of it."

"I do not know the name," Velázquez insisted.

"Of course you don't, you murderer. You didn't care that she was an innocent victim in your filthy drug war, that she came upon your stuff by accident. And you!" Ric's eyes blazed as he glared at Samantha. "The so-great specialist, golden girl of Finders, Inc. You had to get them all, didn't you? You couldn't leave Maria out of it."

"She was a member of a smuggling ring, Ric. I couldn't condone what she'd done, let it go without saying a word. That would have made me complicit in her crime."

"So you set her up in a sting that went bad. Rather like this one, isn't it?" He smiled but it was not pleasant.

"We'll see. Let me finish my story now."

"What do you want them to know, Sam? That I had you running all over the place trying to get your hands on a statue that's long gone."

"That statue was the crux of your con. You couldn't have it surface too soon. Not after you found out there were gold coins to be had. You killed two men, Ric. Was it worth it?"

Everyone's attention was on the man who'd ruined so many lives, but Ric refused to look cowed.

"Where is the statue?" Daniel asked, breaking the silence.

"She's such a good recovery agent, let her find it."

"I will, Ric. And I'll make sure it goes back to where it belongs."

"Wait a minute. He killed two men?" Carlos asked.

"Varga and Sanchez," Sam told him. "Both were tired of playing puppet. Varga was your man, Carlos, but he was also working for Ric. You left after you killed Father Bert, so did Ric, in that plane I heard. But Varga came behind, searching for the coins as Ric had told him to do. I think that later on Varga became afraid you would hear about it, Carlos, but I also think his conscience got to him. He wanted out."

"Sniveling little coward," Ric sneered.

"At least he had a heart. Sanchez only wanted the statue and he was willing to pay for it—twice. Once, just before the cruise." Daniel looked at Carlos. "Shelby found a large amount of money had been transferred from his account to one she's now traced to Ric. Then he paid again, the day he died. Ric promised to have it delivered. Instead he shot Sanchez."

"Sanchez was greedy," Ric muttered. "His home is filled with artifacts but he was always after one more. Greed isn't good."

"Is revenge better?" She took a deep breath, hoped Daniel could take this. "You didn't care about Bert or his work, did you, Ric? You merely used him to steal from Carlos. You'd already stashed the cocaine somewhere. You probably watched while Carlos accused Bert."

"You're the reason my uncle died. You set him up, just as you did Samantha." Daniel's tone was edged with steel. "You've used everybody."

Ric's bravado was cracking under the strain, yet he said nothing.

"Why, Ric?" Samantha burst out. "Tell me why you let an innocent man die."

Ric remained mum.

"I'll explain then, shall I?" She lifted out the cocaine, grabbed a handful of the coins and spilled them from her fingers. "You needed Carlos to scare everyone away from that compound so you could get your drugs. That should have been the end of it. But you had to go back."

"Go back?" Daniel frowned. "Why?"

"Such beauty." Obrigado dropped to his knees, began picking up the disks.

Sam saw Jose move slightly and shook her head. *Not yet.*

"Ric used Obrigado, too. He needed someone to authorize a flight in and out of the jungle quickly, before the authorities came to examine it. Obrigado was to get half of the coins for his trouble."

"But how did he know about them? I didn't even know," Daniel said.

"I'm sure Bert talked about his find during those long trips in and out of the jungle, didn't he?"

Ric smirked. "His treasure, he called it."

"Yes." She paused, staring at Daniel. "The day after Bert died, when I got to the train station, Ric was there. He'd been tracking illegal transport he said, but lost his man. He paid for my ticket back to Lima and while we rode, we talked. He saw the coins, probably guessed then that Bert hadn't given them all to the museum."

"So he had to get you on that cruise so he could go back," Daniel guessed. "That's why he kept feeding you info on the statue, so you'd stay out of his way."

She nodded. "Yes."

"Varga was working for both Carlos and Ric." He towered over Carlos. "Did you pay him to threaten Sam on the cruise?" Daniel's eyes glowed like orange-hot flames.

"It wasn't Varga, it was another of your men, wasn't it, Carlos."

The drug lord shrugged. "He was supposed to scare her so she'd tell him where she'd hidden the drugs."

"And locking us in that room? Drugging Sam? Was that your doing, too?"

Velázquez looked puzzled.

"It was Ric, Daniel. Varga tried to warn me about him but I didn't understand."

"So Ric had the coins and the cocaine all along."

Samantha nodded. "I found them this afternoon at his house. Or rather the home of el Zopilote."

Daniel glared at Ric. "You really are a vulture, aren't you? You prey on everyone."

"You've probably been short on every shipment since you made a deal with the devil," Sam told Carlos. "You never expected that Ric was playing you, that he wasn't your faithful chore boy. You honed in on his suggestion that Bert was the problem and you decided to play God."

"This is—"

"The truth," Sam insisted, chilled by the evil that shot through his eyes. "I saw you that day. I watched you give the order to kill an innocent man. For cocaine." She shook her head sadly. "And all the while you were tearing up the camp for something that wasn't there, Ric was laughing."

"You have no proof I did anything." Velázquez's voice rang cold and hard.

"You caused a man's death," Samantha accused. "I was there, *señor.* I saw you."

"I have ten witnesses who will say they saw me elsewhere." A haughty smile played across the thin lips. "You have no proof, *señorita.* You should be more careful." The threat underlying his words made her shiver.

"I have proof." Jose stepped forward. "Sam phoned me when she got to the train station. A forensic team flew to the site the next day. They found a cigarette butt at the scene of Bert McCullough's death in the jungle. A DNA test should be enough to make her testimony stick, Carlos. You won't wiggle out of this one. It's just too bad we couldn't get there earlier. We would have caught this vulture, too. Get cuffs on them," he ordered his men.

"I've done nothing," Obrigado protested. "You can't arrest me."

"You conspired with Carlos, here and to commit fraud against the government of Peru," Jose snarled. "Legal agreements like the one you signed for those coins are binding. You can't change them just because you're a greedy, grasping man. I've got a long file of corrupt practices that I'm going to enjoy investigating, Obrigado. Get him out of here."

Carlos Velázquez said nothing. He didn't have to. They all knew how long he'd last in jail.

Ric pulled back when he came level with Sam. "I underestimated you," he said softly. "You really are the best there is."

"You used me, Ric. I only wanted to be your friend. I never meant for Maria to die. I'm sorry you didn't know that."

"That doesn't help much, Sam," he mumbled, his face angry. "She's still gone."

"But what you did won't bring her back."

The officer urged him out.

"Jose, I can't thank you enough for helping with this," Sam said as she picked up the coins and returned them to the chest."

"I'll have thanks enough in a couple of months," he joked, winking at her. "For now I'll personally take charge of this chest. Both of you will accompany me back to headquarters. You can give your statements there. Mr. McCullough, we're also going to need your report of kidnapping by Carlos's men. If you'll go with my man he'll take you to the station."

"I'll be along, but first I want to talk to Bertha and her friends, to thank her for helping us," Samantha told him. "And I need to call my office to let them know Daniel's safe."

"Yes, of course. Hector will stay with you and when you are ready he will bring you in." Jose frowned. "I'll expect a full report of this afternoon's incidents. I hope there were no illegal actions taken in locating that chest. I want Carlos Velázquez locked up for a long time."

"It's against the rules for any employee of Finders, Inc. to break the law," she told him with a sideways glance at Daniel. "Besides which, I don't have to stoop to their methods. If you can get a search warrant for Ric's house, you might find the statue there. I'll leave that up to you."

"You did a great job, Samantha." Daniel's voice was for her alone as Jose directed the loading of the chest.

"It was a cooperative effort. Shelby pulled out all the stops, too."

"I know but—" He paused, his mouth tight at the interruption.

"I'm sorry to intrude but we must leave." Jose glanced from one to the other. "It's important to get going on this before the papers get wind of it. I don't want Carlos's lawyer bailing him out."

"We'll talk later, Daniel."

"Count on it." His amber eyes held hers in a promise. "We've got some unfinished business."

Samantha followed Daniel and his guard from the church. Bertha and her friends waited outside. Samantha thanked them profusely. "We'll celebrate at dinner tomorrow evening."

Bertha declined. "Some of us would not be so comfortable at a fine restaurant," she murmured, a touch of pink coloring her cheeks.

"Me, neither. I was thinking of El Palacio de Pollo." The Chicken Palace offered outdoor tables, plenty of food, laughter and fun. No one could feel uncomfortable there.

Bertha's grin widened and she nodded eagerly. *"Sí, señorita. El Palacio de Pollo es muy bueno."*

They agreed on a time to meet, and then Sam left for the station with Hector. On the way she phoned Shelby with the good news.

"You two take a couple of days and relax. There's no need to come rushing back. I'll handle things."

"Thanks, Shelby."

At the station Sam was taken to a small room where she waited a long time before giving her statement. Then came the questions. By the time she was finally allowed to leave, Daniel was nowhere to be seen. Hector dropped her off at the hotel just as the hotel clock struck three in the morning.

Alone in the empty room, Sam pulled open the windows. The fears and doubts she'd felt earlier were gone now. She'd trusted and God had been there. But she couldn't stop thinking about Daniel.

She had too many questions and too few answers. There was no way of knowing what Daniel thought until she talked to him. Until then she needed sleep.

"Sam? Are you here?" Daniel stood in the center of the suite, felt its emptiness.

His spirit plummeted to his shoes.

He sank into a chair, let his head roll back as waves of tiredness washed over him. It was probably a good thing she wasn't here. He was too tired to talk to her anyhow. Jose had been determined they retrace every step of his kidnapping, which meant a long drive out to the palatial estate, finding the room, waiting while pictures were taken, and answering the unending questions. But he'd hung in there because he wanted it over with.

He had plans.

Only Samantha didn't know that. Daniel smiled at his own gullibility. As if she'd be sitting here, waiting for him to appear. Sam wasn't the kind of woman who waited around for anyone. She went out and made things happen.

After he kicked off his shoes and removed his jacket and shirt, he noticed the sheet of hotel stationery fluttering to the floor.

Daniel: Promised Bertha and troupe a feast to celebrate. Feel free to join us; otherwise I'll be back later on. She'd added the address of the chicken place and scrawled her name across the bottom.

He honed in on her signature while his mind created

her likeness—laughing, teasing, grabbing on to life and enjoying it. Like a wave, the tiredness dropped away.

Plans had to be changed, adapted, rethought if you wanted to achieve your goal. That was probably the best thing Samantha had taught him, to stop trying to control everything and relax, change on the fly. He'd done it before, he'd just forgotten.

Daniel shaved, showered and dressed with one goal in mind—to get to Sam. He could hear the boisterous laughter when he walked through the restaurant door. A stooped smiling man showed him to the patio where Bertha and company sat around a huge table. Some had dressed up for the occasion. Their strange and unusual combinations of clothing surprised him, but it was Samantha who sucker punched him.

Tonight she wore a simple white off-the-shoulder blouse with a flounce that showed off her tanned shoulders and the small gold coin that matched his. She was laughing at something unabashedly, head thrown back, shoulders shaking, mouth split in a wide grin. Then she saw him and the smile died.

"*Hola,* Daniel! Come on in. Have a seat. You remember everyone."

"Thanks. I'd like to." Acting on impulse, he walked over to her, brushed a kiss against her cheek then eased between her and Bertha. "This looks like fun."

"Today is a great fiesta," Samantha told him, eyes wide with surprise as she shifted to make room. "We are celebrating."

"Great." The waiter brought him a plate and he helped himself from the huge platters on the table. Bertha shook her head at his portions and added another half chicken to the pile.

A man at the end of the table rose, held out his glass and said in Spanish, "A toast—to our dear Father Bert. He is with us still."

Everyone rose, held their glasses to him in a salute of honor. Daniel rose, smiled at them as his heart wrenched. "To el Padre Dulce," he said quietly. They nodded, sipped, then the meal continued.

Sitting beside her, Daniel was content to watch Sam interact with her new friends. With them she was relaxed and natural. The evening lengthened as the group shared stories of their family who had passed on, days they'd known better times, teasing reminders that none of them could make it on the street without friends. At last Bertha rose and held up her glass.

"One more toast," she said in Spanish, her smile huge as she looked at him. "A toast to Señorita Sam and her *novio*." The others quickly grabbed their cups and rose. Comments about Sam and him were offered loudly and with many sly looks.

Beside him, he felt Samantha tense. Her smile grew tight, forced, and she didn't look at him. Daniel rose, clinked his glass against Bertha's and took a sip. Then he set it down, wrapped an arm about Samantha's waist and pressed a kiss on her lips to the loud applause of the group.

After a moment Samantha eased away from him as if she were shy. But he knew better. He tipped up her chin, met her gaze and said, "Thank you."

"You're welcome." She turned away quickly to speak to Bertha but not before he'd seen the confusion in her eyes.

Bertha and the others were moving from the table—the meal was over. The group gathered around them, shaking hands first with Sam then with him. Then they quietly filed out of the restaurant. Bertha was last.

"You gave us a very happy memory tonight, Señorita Sam, Señor Daniel," she said, her dark face shining. "We will remember this time for many happy years after you have gone away."

"I will remember you, too, Bertha. I'm so glad I met you." Sam hugged her tightly, her heart brimming. "Go with God, Bertha."

"And you." Bertha wrapped her arms around Daniel's neck and pasted a kiss on his cheek, then giggled like a schoolgirl. "He is a good man," she whispered to Sam. Then she opened her capacious bag and pulled out a small box. "This is a gift for both of you. Tonight, when you sit together under the stars together, open it and think of Bertha."

She handed the box to Sam then bustled away, her voice echoing back to them as she chided the others for taking too long to leave.

While Samantha paid the bill, Daniel made sure there was a huge tip on the table. Then he paid for cabs for everyone. Finally he and Sam were alone on the sidewalk.

"What do you think is in it?" Daniel asked, watching her face.

"Bertha makes bracelets. She's probably given us a couple of those." She lifted her head, sniffed the air. "There's a park over there. Do you mind if we walk for a while? The evening is so beautiful."

"Of course." He tucked her hand in his arm and led her across the street. A woman was just packing up her flower cart. Daniel chose three perfect purple orchids and handed them to Sam. "For you. Congratulations on a wonderful job."

"But I failed. I didn't recover the statue."

"You put three men in jail. That's pretty good." He stopped when she did, in front of a fountain, and watched as multicolored lights turned its water into a rainbow.

Daniel dug a coin out of his pocket and tossed it into the water.

"Did you make a wish?" she asked, her voice quiet.

"Yes." He studied her face in the moonlight and suddenly the words he'd struggled to find didn't matter. "Do you want to hear it?"

"You can't tell your wishes or they don't come true." Her warning barely penetrated the night sounds.

"I'm afraid that if I don't tell you mine it will never come true." He faced her, took the brown package and the flowers from her hands and set them on the edge of the fountain, then placed his hands on her shoulders. "I love you, Samantha. My wish is that you meant what you said that day on the phone, that you love me, too."

She didn't flinch, didn't move away. Her steady gaze held his. "I didn't say I loved you," she murmured. "I said 'me, too.'"

"Oh." He forced air into his lungs. "Okay, then. If we went out again, if we took it very slow, if I promised not to push you, do you think—" He had to stop. Her fingers were across his lips.

"What I wanted to say was that I needed you with me, helping me, that I couldn't imagine never seeing you again, never feeling your arms around me, holding me."

"Like this?" he asked as he followed her suggestion.

"Mmm." She wrapped her arms around his neck. "That's almost right."

Almost? He meant to ask about that, but Daniel got caught up in the beauty of her face, the way her green eyes shone in the moonlight, the way her head of curls never seemed to stay still.

"Um, Daniel?"

"Yes?" She had a pert, sassy jaw that promised she'd hold her own in the future.

"You're the risk assessor. What are the chances you're going to kiss me?"

He leaned down, touched her lips with his own. "In basketball terms we call it a slam dunk," he said, then proceeded to kiss her as he longed to.

"I think I love basketball," Samantha whispered after some time had passed. She brushed her hand against his cheek. "I think I've loved you ever since you aimed the water pistol at that poor little duck and missed."

"You didn't show it." He kissed the soft indentation of her cheekbones, the smoothly sculpted jaw, and the corner of her gorgeous mouth. Reality returned. "I'm not good at relationships, Samantha. I've never let myself be fully invested. I let Uncle Bert do the work, just like with Shelby and Grant. I didn't want to be hurt when they left," he admitted. "Everyone I ever cared about has gone away."

"I only went because you sent me here."

He nodded. "I was afraid you'd quit, and I needed time to come up with a new plan to woo you."

She tilted her head to one side. "What's the new plan?"

"It only has one step. I'm going to marry you, Samantha Henderson."

"I see. When?"

At least she hadn't turned him down.

"Does tomorrow work for you?" At her start of surprise, Daniel rushed to explain. "You've had my heart for a long time, Sam. I don't need to wait, I'm positive you're the one God sent for me."

"You're sure it's not just a role you're playing, that you won't get tired of me in a few months?" Doubts flickered over her face.

"Did you ever wonder why everyone on that cruise believed we were a couple? It was because they could see I wasn't playing a part. I love you, have loved you, and will love you. Forever."

"Me, too." She stood on tiptoe and kissed him. "I'd love to marry you in Peru, Daniel. Tomorrow will do just fine." Sam leaned back in his arms, looked heavenward. "I guess you were right after all."

"I was?"

"God did put us together." She drew her arms away, bent to pick up the box and her flowers. "Let's go to the hotel and plan our honeymoon. I've got some holiday time coming and I'm pretty sure my boss will let me off."

"Samantha?"

"Yes?"

Daniel pointed to the package. "We're here, under the stars. Why not see what Bertha sent?"

"Okay." As she perched on the side of the fountain, she handed him her flowers and the string around the package. Then she poked through the newspaper. "Oh, my."

Daniel leaned forward to get a better look. "The statue." He checked the front of the box. "The handwriting says this was to be delivered to Señor Zopilote."

"And the shipper is the same company Ric worked for when the statue was stolen." Sam blinked. "He shipped it to himself?"

"Looks like it. By ground, which is why it took so long. There's a note."

Sam unfolded the paper. "Bertha says her friend went

back for a wrench he'd left at Ric's and found the package lying on the front step. She says I'll know what to do with it."

"It'll have to go to Jose, be cleared by customs and returned to the museum."

"I know." She lifted the statue out, studied it. "Such a small thing, such a lot of trouble. You know what this means, don't you, Daniel?"

Studying her face in the starlight, he didn't much care. But Daniel shook his head as he placed the object back in its protective covering. "No. What?"

"It means I have completed my assignment." Her chin thrust out in that Samantha-way, and her eyes glittered with suppressed excitement. "It means I'm going to ask for that promotion again."

"I'll be happy to hear it—when I'm back in my office. Right now I'm taking my fiancé back to the hotel."

She opened her mouth to respond, but his phone cut her off.

"Hello? Hi, Shelby. We're fine. Listen, I'm sorry to do it to you, but I'm going to be gone a while longer. Probably two weeks." He brushed his lips against Sam's forehead, holding his phone so she could listen. "If you must know, Sam and I are going on a cruise. To the Galapagos Islands."

"Again?"

Daniel looked at Samantha, who burst out laughing.

"Bye, Shelby," they said in unison. Then he closed the phone and turned it off.

They walked down the street, arms entwined, to the nearest taxi stand. But even though Daniel had bartered a price with the driver, Samantha didn't get in. She was too busy staring up at the stars.

"Did you see that?" she whispered, as a flash of light glimmered then disappeared. "A shooting star."

"You think that's what it was?" Daniel hugged her close, breathed in her Persian rose perfume. "I think it was Bert giving us his approval. He always did love firecrackers."

As they rode back to the hotel, a thousand stars blinked on and off in the inky darkness of the heavens above. But Samantha and Daniel didn't even notice.

* * * * *

Dear Reader,

I hope you've enjoyed your second visit with the folks at Finders, Inc. Doesn't Peru sound like a wonderful place? The colors, the history, the majestic splendor of the countryside—each of these continues to fascinate those who visit this marvelous country.

Perhaps it takes getting away from our normal lives to realize how much we have to depend on God and His generosity in loving us. In the rush of everyday life, whirling past the duties we sometimes complete so mindlessly, we often lose sight of how precious His love for us is.

I wish for you a quiet time in the chaos of your life, a time to relax in the peace, comfort and joy of knowing the One who sent His son so you might live.

I love to hear from readers. You can reach me at loisricher@yahoo.com or check out my Web site, www.loisricher.com.

Blessings,

Lois Richer

QUESTIONS FOR DISCUSSION

1. Sam and Daniel were both skilled at assuming other identities. Discuss how this facet of their careers could have a negative impact on the way in which they dealt with their world.
2. Daniel's feelings of guilt stemmed from his childhood and carried into his later life. Share events from your own past that you've dealt with as an adult and if applicable, how God has used those events to teach you.
3. Samantha believed Ric was her friend, yet he turned out to be her enemy. Discuss reasons she wanted to believe in him and how that made her vulnerable to his deception.
4. The gold coins held different meanings for each of the major characters. Suggest the underlying significance of those meanings for Daniel, Samantha and Ric, and how it affected their worldview.
5. The more we interact with people, the more often we make snap judgments about them, from the way they respond to a mild inquiry to their body language or personal hygiene. Early in the story Samantha made a snap judgment about Daniel that seriously affected their relationship. Spend one day noting your own snap judgments about anyone you come in contact with and if possible, find out if they're true.

6. Personalities often change when people move out of familiar surroundings; perhaps they become more adventuresome, or less voluble. Discuss some changes you've noticed in your travels. List some things, positive and negative, that you learned about yourself during that time.

7. Daniel found relationships difficult because he never let himself get too involved in case something went wrong. Many times we do the same thing with God, skimming Scripture instead of digging deep for the answers we want. Consider your personal faith journey. Is your faith a conscious choice, a result of your upbringing or something else?

8. Each of us has enemies that no one else can see. Reflect on your own life and what affects you the most—fear, loneliness, buried anger, dissatisfaction, abandonment or something else, then suggest ways to handle them.

9. Bertha was a tremendous help to Sam and Daniel. Think of someone who helped you in a difficult time, then list ways you can help others.

Love Inspired®

Look for these titles in Lois Richer's romantic suspense miniseries...

FINDERS, INC.

Recovering lost items and mending broken hearts.

SECRETS OF THE ROSE
August 2006

SILENT ENEMY
September 2006

IDENTITY: UNDERCOVER
October 2006

Available wherever you buy books.

Steeple Hill®

www.SteepleHill.com

LISFI

Love Inspired® SUSPENSE

TITLES AVAILABLE NEXT MONTH

Don't miss these two stories in October

IDENTITY: UNDERCOVER by Lois Richer
Finders, Inc.

For Callie Merton, one of Finders Inc.'s best agents, keeping secrets was a way of life. Even when she married fellow agent Max Chambers, she couldn't face her past. But now hidden information was threatening her marriage. Would Callie reveal the truth—and save her marriage—or allow her past to destroy her future?

SEASON OF SECRETS by Marta Perry

As a teenager, Dinah Westlake witnessed her cousin's murder, but blocked the memories. A decade later, her cousin's widower, Marc Devlin, returned home before Christmas, creating an opportunity for family healing. But when several dangerous "accidents" occured, Dinah's recollections began to resurface, putting her back in the path of a desperate killer.

LISCNM0906